FICTION Foxall, Raymond Jehoiada Campbell, 1916-
Brandy for the parson. St. Martin's Press
[1974, c1970] 224p. Bibl. 6.95.

The Little Ferret - Harry Adkins - returns to
solve a murder on the smuggler-infested Romney
Marshes.
1. Adkins, Harry - Fiction.

10,000/78

Raymond Foxall

Brandy for the Parson

NEW YORK
ST. MARTIN'S PRESS, INC.

Five and twenty ponies
Trotting through the dark—
Brandy for the parson;
'Baccy for the clerk;
Laces for a lady; letters for a spy,
And watch the wall, my darling, while
                the gentlemen go by.

RUDYARD KIPLING

AUTHOR'S NOTE

HARRY ADKINS, the central figure in this book, was a living person, one of those earliest of detectives known as Bow Street Runners, and in his day he earned the nickname of The Little Ferret. Sir Richard Ford and John Clark were also persons who existed.

It is true that Napoleon, hoping to invade England, had his spies in Britain and he so relied on English smugglers being the means of intelligence reaching him that he did have the port of Roscoff specially built for those British free-trading captains not perhaps so patriotic as the remainder of their breed during that war with France. It is also true that Bow Street Runners were at that time called in by the customs authorities to investigate particularly bad outbreaks of smuggling, or the murder of revenue men, and by the government to help in matters of national security.

Gangs on the Kent and Sussex coasts running goods to avoid paying duty would often be several hundred strong. They did have armed guards to protect them, were prepared to fight for their contraband and committed outbreaks of violence which struck fear into peaceable folk.

The foregoing facts form the basis of my story.

BIBLIOGRAPHY

Smugglers' Britain, Smuggling Tales From the Past: G. Bernard Wood.

The Smugglers: Picturesque Chapters in the Story of an Ancient Craft: Charles G. Harper.

Smuggling Days: Smuggling in the 18th and 19th Centuries: Katherine Chadsfield.

Autobiography of a Cornish Smuggler: Captain Harry Carter, 1749-1809.

Romney Marsh: Walter J. C. Murray.

King's Cutters and Smugglers: E. Keble Chatterton.

The History of the Bow Street Runners: Gilbert Armitage.

The Story of the Police, Law and Order: (Dumpleton).

New Study of Police History: (Reith).

History of Everyday Things in England: Marjorie and W. H. D. Quennell.

The First Detectives: Belton Cobb.

Leatherface: John Dickson Carr.

Hue and Cry: Birth of the British Police: Patrick Pringle.

The Thieftakers: Patrick Pringle.

Memoirs of a Bow Street Runner: Henry Goddard.

PROLOGUE

OUT IN THE dark and over the sea the wind was rising. Soon it would freshen over the newly-built moorings in the little harbour and rattle the shutters that blinded the latticed eyes of the houses beyond. Rising, it would moan mysteriously over the roofs and whistle ominous, indecipherable messages in the narrow streets of the French port.

Already the gulls were in over the huddled buildings, wheeling and squawking, protesting in their strange, crying calls that further discomfort was to be added to their hunger.

As the first drops of rain spattered the cobbles at his feet, a man wearing a dark cloak and tall-fronted, military hat strutted hurriedly down the seafront and rapped sharply with his cane on a weathered door. He brushed quickly past the man who opened it, spitting a clipped *"Merci!"* from between tight lips. In an upper room he closed the door behind him, removed his cloak, hat and swordbelt, rummaged in a rickety bureau for paper, ink and pen, lighted the three wicks of a candelabra gracing the table and sat down.

His quill scratched and he rose to open the window, gazing out over the old harbour which until a few hours ago had echoed to the ring of hammers and the shouts of workmen. It was too dark to see the result of the operation he had organized there in the past months. But he knew what had been accomplished. The harbour had been widened; additional stone steps led down to the water; extra mooring rings, as yet unrusted, lined the wharf.

In the dim light he could see the furled sails of perhaps

a dozen luggers and cutters. There was room now for many more!

This would please certain furtive captains who sailed in from the Channel and for whom these new berths were intended. Most of all it would gratify the great Napoleon Bonaparte, master of France and this officer's eventual superior, who cast greedy eyes across the sea to England.

The man at the window was an important link in the chain of the emperor's ambition. For Colonel Jean-Paul Boussant had been sent to this port of Roscoff by Bonaparte himself to organize alterations to the harbour and remain there in charge of an operation dear to the emperor's heart.

Through the open casement he could see the screaming gulls. In the grey night they were like flying ghosts, dipping their lost white souls in blackest limbo.

The town prepared itself for sleep. The lights went out, one by one. The squalls came in at last, blurring the harbour and its rocking masts. Over the wind the voice of the sea-birds rose, more and more insistent, and for a single moment the man at the window imagined that their cries bore a message that could not be translated. . . .

He smiled at the thought, for he of all Frenchmen knew that there *were* to be messages, very important ones, coming across the Channel in the pockets of those cunning captains, written in letters or whispered in the ear. And all because of the work he had started in the harbour at Roscoff. . . .

For that work was only the beginning of the secret military assignment entrusted to him by Napoleon I of France. Now his real task would begin, and Boussant was the man to see it through.

When the war with Britain had begun in 1793 he had relinquished an artillery command to begin a study of intelligence methods. Twice then in eleven years he had been smuggled into England as a spy, returning each time with his life, and the enemy none the wiser.

Recognized as an expert in the intelligence service, he it was who now despatched others across the Channel on the darkest nights, sent them messages and awaited their reports. . . .

He waited now . . . smiling thinly, hating the English because they were not yet conquered, but patient in his excessive pride and his personal ambitions.

For Bonaparte, as well he knew, had every confidence in him, and not merely because they had passed together through the army schools in Brienne and Paris. At 35 Boussant had prematurely grey hair, but the French emperor associated it with hardness and tempered steel.

Boussant returned to the table and finished writing his letter. It was addressed directly to Napoleon Bonaparte, and this is what he had penned :

> *I have to inform your highness that the work at the harbour here, which you ordered to be done, is completed, and there is now plenty of room for the English smugglers to come in. There are many new berths for their vessels, and they may remain here so long as they desire.*
>
> *At your personal command, I shall see to it that they are made very welcome, and that they are allowed to purchase brandy and fine articles cheaply so long as they pay for them with guineas, as we require all the gold we can get into our country from England.*
>
> *In addition, I shall see to it that in return for our generosity they bring secretly out of England certain other items, including newspapers, letters from our friends—and at times our friends themselves.*
>
> *It is indeed the only way we can get our agents across and have them returned to us.*
>
> *Rest assured that the port will be maintained as from now as a refuge for those English smugglers who remain friendly towards us.*

The writer sealed the letter and entrusted its despatch to no less than a subaltern.

"Ride without delay to Paris," he ordered. "Place this in

the hand of no other than his Highness the Emperor Napoleon—and do not, if you value your commission and your life, allow any man but he to take it from you."

When the subaltern had gone Boussant sat down and allowed himself some warming thoughts. It was certainly a great year. Napoleon had become emperor. His campaigns continued. He had begun at last real plans to invade Britain. Across the Channel, Mr. William Pitt, who had resigned office three years before, had just returned to power because Bonaparte's threat of invasion had become very real. All this in 1804.

The master spy rose and stood beside the open window, his face towards England, remembering what Napoleon had said to him across a long, polished table in Paris. . . . "It is on the smugglers of England I place my faith. Without them I have no word from that country, no intelligence, no letters, no journals—nothing. Nor do I have gold, which in this war is at a premium, unless they pay for their contraband with English guineas.

"If ever we are to invade their country we must welcome as many of their captains as are unpatriotic, give them a safe port to themselves—and even, if it be necessary, build ships for them."

Boussant closed the window. Suddenly the raucous voices of the gulls had grown much too urgent, grating harshly on his thoughts.

CHAPTER ONE

THE RIDING OFFICER, making haste with what he had
to tell, took the road down the Kent coast at a brisk canter.
Every now and then, and without a moment's thought, he
cut off on an unfrequented track to shorten his journey, for
he was as familiar with the twisting paths and hiding places
as the smugglers he was set to catch.

The Romney marshes lay on his right hand as he rode,
and from time to time the sea sparkled to his left. Continuing
on his way to the coast watch house at Dungeness, he reined
in his horse instinctively at one particular cove. In the light of
day it was as peaceful as any in England, innocent of sound
save for the distant surge of the tide. By the moon it could
be a-bustle with a hundred men.

Ransome Quested, the preventive man, had seen it both
ways. He knew its every stone and pebble. By day he had
done his patrols. In the dark he had watched the gangs at work,
toiling up out of the bay like an army of ants, one man in
hiding and a hundred down there on the strand.

But things were different now, what with the war with
France. There wasn't half the smuggling, and if there were
then there wouldn't be enough revenue men to deal with
it.

Indeed, it would seem there was quite a truce between the
Kent and Sussex contrabanders on the one hand and the excisemen on the other, and it bid fair to last as long as the war did.

"Takes old Boney to stop the night runs," chuckled many
a known smuggler, raising a tankard with a riding officer. "Us
be all Englishmen, eh?"

Well did Quested know "the gentlemen", as they were dubbed, who would seem these days to be putting him out of a job.

He raised his eyes from the beach and gazed over the sea to France. It was across there at Boulogne, they said, that Napoleon had moored his flotillas to invade Britain.

"When will they come?" he said to himself. The words were on everyone's lips.

He raised a hand to his forehead, shielding his eyes against the glare of the sun, as though he could see over the watery miles to the impatient armada riding at anchor at the French coast.

His lips curved in a grin, but it scarcely lightened the long, craggy face. Ransome Quested, an apothecary by trade, was a serious man. That was why, as a riding officer, he was a little different from the breed, who were recruited mostly from the less conscientious or educated, who rode only when their ordinary business allowed it, and wrote down false returns about the patrols they claimed to have made.

Quested was, in consequence, well thought of by the revenue men. For he had more time than most to write out lists of the patrols he had made.

Of course, there was a good reason why he had more time. He must have prospered in the apothecary business, for he had two assistants to look after his shop in Dymchurch, and he could be on the road when he wished.

A highly respected figure was Ransome Quested. For a start he was of build tall and imposing. And then, his riding boots and cravats were of the best, and in church of a Sunday he might have been the squire himself, so fashionably turned out was he for a countryman.

And folk got used to his dourness. It was in keeping, they said, with a worthy shopkeeper, if not a riding officer.

The smile that now softened that gravity came because what he had to tell was to do with those fears of invasion. He turned his horse's head out of the wind that blew from France.

Soon he was at the look-out post of Dungeness and in conference with the officer in charge, Lieutenant Hogan.

"Have you seen any strangers through your telescope?" asked the visitor.

"As a riding officer, you'll be referring to the free traders, eh?" returned the lieutenant. "If you are, Mr. Quested, I've got more important vessels on my mind—vessels manned by the French devils."

"The same I'm thinking of, lieutenant."

"Oh well, Frenchies aren't much your concern, your job being with the free traders."

"You are quite wrong, Mr. Hogan. It is true I am not a military man, but if little Mister Napoleon invades this coast, then it'd be very much my concern—as an Englishman."

The naval man smiled wryly. "What's on your mind, Mr. Quested?"

"Well, sir, there'd appear to be an offer to help if the French do come. 'Tis a strange offer, but I'm assured 'tis there if you want it."

"Out with it mister. I'm a busy man these days. Who offers help?"

The visitor caught the officer's glance and held it. "The smugglers of Dymchurch."

"The *smugglers*?"

"That is what I said."

"Well, well. The war's turned things arse about face, to be sure it has. How do you know this?"

Quested allowed himself the briefest smile. "The parson told me. 'Tis he suggests it."

"*Parson,* eh? Gets stranger and stranger, don't it? Some parson, eh?"

"You could say that, Mr. Hogan. You could indeed. Man o' many parts is Parson Honeycombe. As tall as a tree and broad as an ox, with a voice like blacksmith's doom. Bit of a fighting man, I'd say, if he got properly roused."

Lieutenant Hogan perched himself on a stool and folded his

arms. "Sounds like a bit of a fellow-me-lad, this parson. Counts the odd smuggler among his friends, eh?"

"The *odd* one, Mr. Hogan? That's a laugh. Every man in his choir has handled more casks than the excisemen themselves. I *know* that they never make a run without leaving a keg o' the best brandy behind his gate. And I wouldn't be surprised if he hadn't watched them at it times."

"Meaning, Mr. Quested?"

"Meaning nothing. But let me tell you what parson said. He took me on one side as I came out of church on Sunday and said the free traders were sharpening their cutlasses and priming their muskets. 'What for, parson?' I says. 'To make a run with the brandy?' 'The Lord be praised, no,' he says. 'To throw the French back in the sea if they show their faces here.'"

The lieutenant was smiling. "You are beginning to interest me," he said.

"Aye, that's how the parson spoke out. Said he'd offer his whole choir in the eventuality. Them and more, fifty all told. But listen to this—said he'd take charge of 'em and lead 'em himself against the French."

"That's a laugh."

"It is no such thing. Ever seen him?"

"Can't say I have."

"Could throw you over a gate with one hand, that he could."

"Ah!"

There was a moment's silence.

"Just thought it my duty to tell you."

"You did right to speak out. Now let me see, I'm just wondering if we can trust such men."

"I do not think you know the smugglers of Dymchurch. The parson says they are decent men, who but take peacefully what they feel to be their due, all on account of the heavy taxes, you understand. They are but the free traders—or *fair* traders, as they prefer to be known. Vicar Honeycombe says they've sworn not to smuggle a single cask until the war is over."

"Not talking much like a riding officer—not at this precise moment, eh?"

"I'm talking like an Englishman who does not want the Frenchies landing here and making free of my shop. However, if I'm wasting my time——"

"Wait! I didn't say that. Would they follow your parson?"

"Follow him? They have a great respect for him. Do anything he said. Think they're afraid of him, too. He in his turn knows them for what they are—just mortal men like the rest of us and struggling to live. A gatherer of lost souls is our parson. And besides, like I said, they leave him a little something at his gate."

"Mr. Quested, my thanks to you. If the French do come we'll want every cutlass we can lay our hands on—and arms to use 'em. I shall forward your idea to the authorities. Come to think of it, the idea isn't all that strange. I've already heard of something like it. They do say that in other parts the free traders have joined forces for the duration with the preventive men—and are using their ships to help patrol the coast—aye and with they who used to be their enemies. Strange what a war can do, eh?"

"It is quite remarkable. Smuggling's not so cut-throat nowadays, and the days of the gangs, leastways not the desperate ones—I'm thinking of the old Hawkhurst Gang, which you'll remember—would seem to be quite over."

"But not all their murders and killings are solved. However, we must be glad of the offer that has come to your ears."

The two shook hands on the matter, and the riding officer set off to return to Dymchurch, where Vicar Honeycombe would no doubt be pleased to learn that his patriotic idea had been taken in a right and proper spirit. Several times on the way Quested halted his horse and looked across the sea to France.

* * *

It was, as Lieutenant Hogan had said, remarkable what strange things a war could bring about. For that night a well-muffled figure waited at a lonely inn down the coast near St. Mary's Bay to take part in a different sort of conversation.

He had come in out of the gusty dark with his hat pulled down over his eyes, and the high collar of his coat about his ears to keep a voluminous scarf in place beyond his nose. No one in the place, therefore, saw his face, nor remembered ever having seen the fellow.

He who was to meet him would know him by his voice and where he would be sitting. For he, too, had never seen the stranger's features.

The man who waited withdrew his huge bulk into a far alcove, choosing a spot to which the lamps' glow reached out dying fingers. The tankard of ale for which he had growled lay untouched before him on the table, and he averted his eyes from any who might address him.

A quarter hour passed before the door opened to the shriek of the wind and a dark-bearded individual wearing a high-necked jersey and weathered navy-blue jacket. He latched the door behind him, swept off a thick woollen cap and peered at once into the shadowy corner.

"H'ah, Bart Barley, a wild 'un tonight." The landlord of *The Floating Light* intercepted him as he strode towards the silent stranger. "You ain't brought your ship in on a night like this?"

"Came in this morning," replied the seaman, pausing. "Was quite calm then."

"H'ah," said the landlord. Then, as the new arrival passed on, he winked knowingly to the men sitting around his fire and added in quieter tones: "Best look after your new ship, cap'n."

His customers returned the wink, for all were at a loss to know where Bartholemew Barley had got the money to buy that fine, two-masted lugger he now skippered.

"You're late," were the words that greeted Barley as he joined the solitary figure in the corner.

"Aye, sir. I'm sorry."

It was to be the only part of their conversation that would be overheard, for both proceeded to lower their voices.

"Well, did you go to the port I told you to?" demanded the man who had waited, speaking from the folds of his large muffler.

"Yes, I went to Ros——"

"Hold your tongue!" hissed the stranger. "I have told you. Do not utter the name."

"Aye, aye, sir. Sorry, sir."

"Remember it then, and do as I say, for you are much beholden to me."

"Aye, sir." Barley's eyes fell as his companion's glinted coldly above the masking scarf, and an interrogation of the seaman began.

"Did you run into any trouble?"

"None, sir. There ain't many revenue cutters a-lookin' for us these days, on account o' they're mostly on naval work again."

"Was it as I said?"

"It was. It's a grand little harbour, and made special for the likes of English captains who follow—er, a certain trade."

"Precisely."

"And a merry welcome and all. Took me to one o' Boney's officers——"

"Have a care, Barley, or I shall be forced to put a less talkative fellow in charge of the ship. Maybe you realize now why I keep from you my identity. You'd shout that from the masthead, too. Please to remember. Speak no name of place, person or country. Certainly not in a tavern, which has four walls—for walls have ears."

"Aye, aye, sir. As I was saying, sir, I was taken to this man—and a fine gentleman he was and all. Poured me his best claret. Said there was all I could carry of brandy and baccy, laces and silks, all at reasonable prices, allus provided it were paid fer in the manner he wished——"

"Which was with gold."

"Aye, guineas."

"Excellent. I shall see you get a good supply o' them. And did he tell you—anything else?"

"Aye, he did."

"Then perhaps you will acquaint me of it." A warning finger was raised. "But pray be careful how you choose your words, and do not try my patience."

"I'll try, sir. The gentleman, he said he hoped his confidence would grow in me."

"And if it did?"

"If it did, then he'd maybe give me something else to carry home besides baccy and brandy, things that 'ud need no hulking about and 'ud slip as easy as a 'andkerchief into a man's pocket. And 'ud be paid for."

"Letters!" hissed the nameless one, leaning a trifle forward and speaking in the lowest tones. "Letters, eh?"

"Correct. Who'd they be for?"

"How should I know, Barley? I'm an Englishman and don't know—nor care a penny—what they're up to over there." The man inclined his head in the direction of the sea. "For my part, there's money in them, and that's all that matters. But if they're all that anxious to correspond with people in this country, then I'll wager there's good money in it for us. What do you say, Barley?"

"I say as I've a fair notion wot it's all about, and I'll not say more'n that." The sly-eyed skipper fingered his cheek, stroking an old cutlass wound that made his features a shade uglier than they might have been.

"I see," whispered his companion. "But do you not think you could shut your eyes to what you think? Do you not believe we might do something for *them* in return for the brandy, specially these days when the—er, postal service is difficult for them?"

"Well, maybe what they're doing ain't none o' my business—and aye, sir, I think we could. If we don't ask no questions, why—we won't get told no lies."

"You are a sensible man."

Barley drained his glass. "But I do feel you have the advantage o' me."

"That, my good Barley, is precisely the way I would have it." The man seemed positively to leer behind his muffled secrecy. "Is there any way in particular I have you at a disadvantage—besides the obvious one?"

"Well, sir, I don't even know your name, nor can guess it, spite of what you know of me——"

"If you'd have a name, Barley, you may have one. Call me if you like, what shall we say—Adams?"

"There's a mighty lot o' Adams in these parts," said the seaman.

"That, Barley, is why I chose it. Call me Adams—and with pleasure."

"But it ain't yer proper name," grumbled the skipper, ill at ease.

"As to that, Barley, you must make up your own mind. I shall leave you now, but with a warning. Breathe one word of our business and I shall tell the authorities what I know about you. They would, I feel, be most grateful—and delighted to get their hands on you."

The skipper blanched beneath his black beard, and his companion, enjoying the sight, continued in even tones: "We shall meet tomorrow, but not here, for I do not wish to be seen with you so soon again in the same place. Please to go to the old windmill near Redman's Cove at nine of the evening prompt."

The man who called himself Adams rose very tall in the shadows, arranging his muffler, hat and high collar with great care, and began to stride out, answering the landlord's "Goodnight, sir" with a curt reply, putting a hand to the latch and letting in one furious gasp of the wind's voice. The next moment the door was slammed, shutting out the night, and the strange figure had gone.

CHAPTER TWO

VICAR HONEYCOMBE was summoned to Dungeness within the week. He went sedately, as befitted his cloth, plodding slowly on a peaceable nag, but one large enough to carry his weight.

He was given due welcome by Lieutenant Hogan, who shook him warmly by the hand and showed him to the most comfortable chair in the watch house.

"I was much intrigued by your proposition, sir," began the officer when the pleasantries were over.

"Thank you," returned the cleric, offering a beautifully chased snuff-box of foreign design. "I but thought it common sense, the French being almost at our throats."

Hogan's eyes twinkled. "I must admit," he said, accepting a pinch of snuff, "that at first I was a little taken aback at the thought. To be honest, sir, I had my doubts about employing a gang of—shall I say ruffians?"

The parson's eyes, which were deep and searching, smiled in return. "So was I," he agreed. "So was I when it was suggested to me. But is it not true that ruffians can give a good account of themselves when it comes to a fight? Pray God, of course, it may never come to that."

"So—it was put to *you*? You are not, then, the author of the idea?"

"I am not."

"It would begin to seem, Mr. Honeycombe, that no one in particular claims responsibility for the offer. In the first place a Mr. Quested says he heard it from you. Now you suggest you got the idea from someone else. Who, then, did think of the idea?"

"Certain men of my parish?"

"The smugglers of your parish, vicar?"

"I would not put it so strongly, lieutenant. They have been known in the past to trade in—er, a manner not quite within the law."

"Whichever way you put it, vicar, I think we understand each other. I am sure we speak of the same type of fish."

The parson was supremely confident. He sat smiling, his strong hands clasped together on his lap. "Shall we just say— *the gentlemen?*"

"To be sure. 'Tis the term used by they who fear the free traders and look the other way when they pass."

Honeycombe's smile vanished, and for the briefest moment his face was not that of the benevolent parson. "*I* am not afraid of them. I have God at my side."

"I did not fancy," said Hogan, "that you did."

"But they fear *me*—as I pray they fear God."

"Excellent! Then they will do your bidding?"

The vicar, who was smiling again, inclined his head in a slow nod.

"Then I should tell you," continued the officer, "that I have spoken to the authorities on the matter, and they are well disposed to the idea."

"I am glad of it. Should the French be sighted, my village must play its part."

"*Your* village, vicar?"

"'Tis mine—spiritually."

"I see. You talk of your spiritual duties. You are not afraid that it might be—er, unusual for a man of the cloth to take up arms, only supposing the need arises."

"The Church has fought for what is right in the past. It will do so again."

"Well that settles it." Hogan offered a jar of tobacco and a selection of clean clay pipes. "Now tell me, when might you have these men ready for inspection?"

"They are not joining the army," put in the vicar quickly.

"No, but they are to be a reserve force for a small piece of the coast near their village. I'd say it is not too much to ask that we know what they are like."

"Of course you may see them, lieutenant. I can have them drawn up on the village green."

"When?"

"I shall give the matter some thought."

"I should like to ride over five days from now. It would be a most convenient date."

"Impossible. 'Tis not a convenient time for me. There are affairs requiring my attention."

"Why, vicar, 'tis not the Sabbath?"

"No, 'tis not. But I have other things to do apart from preaching. Certainly not five days from now. This day week—and no sooner."

"As you wish, then. This day week."

Clenching hands on the matter, the Reverend John Wyndham Honeycombe mounted and moved off, and Lieutenant Hogan raised quizzical eyebrows as he watched him go. For the man who jogged away on the docile cob seemed an unlikely fellow for a cleric, and the officer, noting his firm seat and easy manner, fancied he could handle a more spirited animal should the need arise.

*   *   *

Exactly five days later, the very date the vicar had declined for an inspection, the lugger skippered by Bartholomew Barley hove to beyond sight of the coast and waited for the dark.

Lieutenant Hogan did not, of course, see the vessel for she kept well out of sight. If he had he would have questioned why the *Kentish Maid*, based on the East Road coast and drifting in fine weather, did not come in at once. As it was, he was to ponder later on whether one of the parson's statements, and the events of that night, were not a whit more than coincidence.

But Barley and his like—those of the shady captains who

still sailed with secret cargoes during wartime—were having it all their own way. If the majority of the revenue cutters had been chasing his kind instead of looking for signs of invasion, such furtive masters could have fallen foul of Mr. Pitt's ten-year-old Hovering Act.

The Dymchurch skipper planted his feet wide against the rolling of his deck and smiled as he recalled the words of that act. . . . "Any vessel hovering within three miles of the coast having aboard spirits in casks smaller than 60 gallons, and every vessel of 60 tons or under carrying any wines, tea or coffee is to be forfeited."

Mr. Pitt, that enthusiastic politician, had in addition made shooting at naval officers or revenue patrols at last punishable by death. But Willian Pitt—and his preventive men—were for the time being occupied by events of somewhat greater importance. . . .

So it was for the same reason Barley smiled that others who did not go to sea waited for him with more confidence than they had done for years.

One was a man wearing a jersey and sweat-grimed necker-chief over which was drawn a smock that was traditional for other pursuits than those of a farm labourer. Tying his horse to a post at the rickety door of a disused windmill, he went inside, lit a hurricane lamp and settled himself as comfortably as possible on a barrel drawn up to one of the windows. Then, rubbing a clear space on the dust-dimmed panes, he settled down to watch the sea.

As the light died a wind was born. It came from somewhere over the darkening waves, blowing in on a northerly course, freshening as it rose to brush the cliff tops and comb sleek partings in its green hair.

When it had hurled itself up and over some of its life was spent, and its lost voice moaned on in the solitudes of gorse and stunted tree. It did not tell of a gale to come, for it neither shrieked nor screamed, and its message was neither of life nor death, but of some strange inevitability that folk abroad on the twilit downs would sense but find impossible to understand.

This was the effect it had on the man in the smock when its invisible force, missing nothing on the sweeping downs, encompassed the lonely windmill in its sorrowful symphony. The sails above the watcher's head creaked four times to every groan.

The man who sat alone eased himself into a new position, and began to wish, for no known reason, that the thing for which he waited would occur quickly, before the ageing evening slid easily into night.

"That be 'e!" he breathed aloud at last, as though he had silent company in the old windmill.

An unmistakable series of flashes winked out there to sea. They died abruptly, were repeated three times and expired decisively.

The countryman slid from the barrel, grabbed his lantern and went out into the wind. He looked all around furtively, then swung his light from side to side and raised it aloft three times. Opening the side of the lantern, he then allowed the wind to douse its flame and deposited it inside the windmill.

Untying his horse, he leapt thankfully to the saddle and the thudding of hooves on the half-hard earth provided drum-beat and rhythm to the music of the wind.

In Dymchurch the rider went to a cottage at its farthest end and belaboured urgently on the door. A woman in a white bonnet opened it, and the visitor blurted: "Where be Simon? I wants 'im urgent."

Simon, who was the village fiddler, came to the door in his shirt sleeves and the visitor spoke briefly behind the palm of his hand.

The fiddler jammed a tweed hat on his head, threw a coat about his shoulders, grabbed his violin in its case and hurried out.

He made for the nearest inn, whose lamp-lit windows glowed across the street, and in the parlour put his fiddle to his chin

and drew his bow across the strings to play the opening bars
of a tune the words of which proclaimed :

> *Oh, but ye've been long away*
> *Ye're welcome back again.*

As he placed the instrument back in its case, the tavern's
customers, almost to a man, put down their pots and made for
the door. Outside they dispersed rapidly to carry the message
to others.

The Ship. The Ocean Inn. The City of London. In each
tavern Simon repeated his snatch of music. Then he climbed to
to the crupper of the horse ridden by the man in the smock,
and was taken in haste to every country hostelry within miles.

It was not long before a sizeable force of men had assembled.
Some were in the saddle, others at the reins of horse-drawn
carts, and large numbers on foot. They made no attempt to
skirt the village, but marched and rode down the high street.
Every man seemed to know precisely what was afoot. No
questions were asked, not a command was given. This was no
military operation, yet in the night there was the glint of steel,
and many a musket was gripped in a strong hand.

With the absence of human voices, the scuff of boots and
the clop of hooves on the cobbles made a dead, unearthly
sound, and the good folk of Dymchurch closed their doors
and shutters and pretended that nothing was happening.

The straggling lines of men moved out on to the country road
in the direction of St. Mary's Bay. On the dark road beyond
the town other groups waited. The cavalcade had not travelled
two miles before it was 300 strong.

There were farm labourers and tradesmen who carried no
weapons. They would toil on a beach under the scant light of
stars, and for this night's work each would receive eight shillings—and be well pleased. The men with cutlasses and
muskets would guard them as they worked—and then the
packhorses as they moved off afterwards with their loads.

They did not know as they marched that an alert midshipman, looking from his post seven miles away, had seen the lantern signal that had been made from the windmill and pin-pointed its position to within a reasonable degree of accuracy.

*   *   *

The cove below the windmill was alive with moving figures. They swarmed down the winding cliff paths and moved out towards the boats that Bartholomew Barley had sent off heavily laden from the *Kentish Maid*, lying inshore and directly opposite.

There were two ship's boats and they still floated near the beach, but they were soon dragged clear of the water. From these craft the labourers began at once to hump barrels, casks and boxes, and as they worked the men who carried weapons formed around them a protective semi-circle and strained their eyes to the cliff's top.

After a time, the boats set off to return for more loads to the long, dark shadow that was the *Kentish Maid*. Swiftly, silently as they waited, the little army of free traders carried the contra-band further up the beach and into a rocky inlet which could be seen neither from the coast road nor the sea.

It was an ideal spot for a man who wished to keep a secret. Any who did not know the place like his own garden could look at it from the beach itself and dismiss it as a shallow fissure in the cliff-face. Once inside, however, one found oneself in a veritable cave which even in daylight was bathed in shadow. The place was wide and dry, yet high above was only a narrow strip of sky.

The gang's leader, whoever he was, must have known this coast like his own house to have chosen the little bay.

Madman's Cove they called it. Some there were who still gave to it its older name—Redman's Cove, after the man who built the windmill on the downs above it. *They* were the folk who did not believe the legend from which the new name sprang—or did not care for it. For the story went that in the days before any could remember this Redman character had committed a murder in the windmill, then raced wildly to the cliff's edge and flung himself on to the rocks below.

The windmill, they said, had never been used since.

The statement, it would seem, was not quite true, because now, for the second time that night, its musty lower room was occupied by a solitary figure. This man did not wear a smock, but a long, black greatcoat with a high collar and a dark, high-crowned hat. This time the man who lurked in the old building was the man who called himself Adams. And this time he did not rely on a voluminous muffler to conceal his identity; he wore a black mask.

He surveyed the activities as far as he could see them from the distance, and in the dark, knowing every detail of what passed down there beside the luminous, oily sea, on the trampled sand and in the cavernous storehouse below the cliffs. In his sinister black and with his dark smile, he was like an evil genius presiding from above and afar.

*   *   *

The midshipman, whose name was Harrington, took four men and set off round the coast towards the area where he had seen the signal. It would take him a long time, for he had but recently been drafted to this shore post and did not know the terrain.

After he had gone his superior officer, to whom he had reported the incident, sent out signals at regular intervals. If some naval sloop answered, he would ask her to alter course and search the sea for some miles out.

Meanwhile, Midshipman Harrington made his way round the coast. He judged the light had appeared a distance of six or seven miles as a bird would fly, but that on the roads he might have to travel nine or ten. He went on in silence.

*   *   *

Back at Madman's Cove, Bartholomew Barley had come ashore with the last load of "moonshine", leaving instructions

*with the mate to weigh anchor and make off the moment the
empty boat returned to the ship.*

*Most of the gang had now left the beach, and on the cliff
top men tightened the girths of loaded packhorses and filled
carts with kegs of brandy. As they toiled, the armed men—
"scouts" as they were called, each of whom would that night
earn 20 shillings—tightened their grip on musket and blunder-
buss. For gradually the night clouds were dispersing, and suddenly the moon sailed free. All around tree and bush were no
longer shadows darker than the night, but distinct outlines in
the paler light.*

*In the tradition of the old smuggling gangs, they were pre-
pared to fight for their prize, to which in their quaint way they
believed they had every right.*

At last the midshipman halted his men. The moonlight
showed the outline of a bay not half a mile ahead. It also
revealed, in the distance, the lonely windmill. Its black arms
seemed to hang on it like a gigantic black spider, and it stood
pale and ghostlike in the silver light. But there was, fancied
the young officer, something else. . . .

"The windmill yonder," he said. "Can any man of you see
a glow—one such as a lanthorn would make—in a window
near the ground?"

"Aye, sir," came the reply. "I'd say ye're right, sir."

"Come on," said the officer, moving forward.

*In the moonlit cove Barley left the men to unload the
last cargo, and began to make his way up the winding, treacher-
ous cliff-path. He gained the summit, took a last glance behind
him and began to make for the windmill, for there was something he had to deliver in person.*

Midshipman Harrington and his men reached the end of the
bay and peered down. One glance was enough to realize what
was afoot. The casks and boxes of the last load were clearly

visible in the grip of men toiling up the beach. A boat moved from the beach, its oars dripping silver, making for a ship at the mouth of the cove.

All Harrington knew about her was that she was a two-masted lugger, for even a telescope would not have revealed her name.

Moving his gaze further round, the officer saw a solitary figure walking from the cliff top towards the windmill.

"Men," he ordered, "get to the top of the cliff-path and cut those fellows off. I'm for the windmill first. I'll be with you as soon as possible. Now off with you as quietly as you know how, quiet as mice!"

The midshipman walked softly on the grass. It was as he almost reached the windmill that he caught sight for the first time of scores of ponies and carts and hundreds of men—a massive party ready to vanish like ghosts on the secret paths of Romney Marsh. Their voices echoed uncomfortably close, and they were not by any means the spirits of the night.

The officer took cover behind some gorse bushes. But the man he followed had reached the windmill, to be joined by another who stepped from the doorway to greet him—and dwarfed his sturdy figure as he did so.

"I have brought more than brandy and tobacco from over there." The words drifted clearly on the night air to the officer. "I have also one of those letters you spoke of."

"I fancied you might." The new voice was deep, and it had a note of resonant authority. "Hand it over."

The letter changed hands and disappeared into a deep coat pocket.

The cavalcade was beginning to move off. The voices sounded even nearer. But the midshipman rose and walked forward. Suddenly for Adams and Barley he stepped solidly out of the shadows.

"I will take that letter, sir," he said, "if you don't mind."

"But I do, Mr. Midshipman. I mind very much."

"In the name of the King," declared the officer, "hand it over."

"In the name of fiddlesticks, have this instead——"

The flash and explosion came instantly on Adams's words as a pistol gleamed suddenly in his hand.

The young midshipman crumpled to the ground. Adams, who had fired at point-blank range, knew that he was dead. Without another glance at the still figure, he began to untie his horse from a post near the windmill.

"Lord save us, but you've done it now!" gasped Barley, his jaw sagging.

"Of course I've done it. I had to. He heard what you said. You should have kept your mouth shut and the letter in your pocket until we were miles from here. I really do not know, Barley, what to do with you."

"But what are you going to do? There'll be hell to play——"

"I'm going to get away from here, that's what I'm going to do—and you with me. There might be more of these meddling fools around." So saying he was in the saddle, demanding that Barley mount behind him, putting spurs to the animal as it bore its double load across the downs, and putting the dead man behind them as quickly as he could.

Let the world grow old and wise, men would go on smuggling. But the authorities had thought to have put down the gangs and their murdering ways, these many years. The Hawkhurst Gang had come and gone. And had not Mr. Pitt nine years ago sent a regiment of foot to Deal to burn all the smugglers' rowing boats when they were laid up during stormy weather?

But it would soon be known that a gang in the old mould had appeared. As Barley had said, there would be hell to play.

CHAPTER THREE

WHEN THE MIDSHIPMAN had made for the windmill, the four ratings moved quickly to the top of the cliff-path, making use of every scrap of cover afforded by bush and hedge. Here they stood in line, levelling their muskets at the point where the free traders would appear from below, straining upwards with their last load.

In less time than it takes for a man to count twenty the first wool-capped heads appeared some distance below. The moonlight did not pick out their faces, for the smugglers had blackened them. But their boots clumped on the stony path, and the vanguard carried not kegs but fire-arms that glinted in the night.

"'Alt!" shouted the senior rating. "'Alt—or we fire."

"'Alt be damned! Bastard blockaders! Kiss our arses, revenue bastards!" The derisive cries came seconds before the gang fired their weapons. Their aim was upwards, and the volley went harmlessly over the heads of the sailors. But it alerted the armed men at that moment falling in behind the loaded packhorses.

The four ratings were not aware of this the main body of the smugglers until, preparing to return the fire of the men coming up the path, shots rang out at their backs.

Quickly they realized that in a moment they would be sandwiched between two parties of smugglers, and they raced to one side, seeking cover behind a belt of hawthorns. From behind this screen they fired, re-loaded and fired again. But they were hopelessly outnumbered, and all they could hope to do was make the loading of the last casks an uncomfortable business for the smugglers, who in turn kept shooting until the carts and ponies were on their laden way.

The smugglers' fire was punctuated by the most filthy oaths, blasphemy and mocking shouts. "Creeping Jesuses! God's bastard sods! Mind yer own bloody business, and we'll mind ours. Come out in the open, you arse-creeping customs sods, and we'll shoot you in the blasted codpiece. Tell your bloody Mr. Customer he's a pox-faced swine. We ain't a-feared o' *'im*. Wot's 'is 'e can keep, but wot's ours we'll bloody fight fer."

Their foul-mouthed cries faded as their closely guarded cavalcade moved farther and farther from the coast.

At last all was quiet, and the ratings made at once for the windmill. They found their officer's body sprawling head-down in the long grass, with a huge, deep wound in the chest which told at a glance that he had been shot from very close range. His right arm still clutched his pistol—and this, they found, had not been fired.

The large company of smugglers, they knew, had not moved off in the direction of the windmill, and they had only seen one figure besides that of their officer moving towards it. This, then, had not been the result of any pitched battle.

"It's murder," said one of the sailors in a low, tense voice. "It's bloody murder, that's wot it is."

"Aye," agreed another. "Aye, and we'll bloody tell 'em."

They carried the body to where they had left the horses and with tree-branches and their jackets made a stretcher to sling between two of the animals.

This was their Mr. Midshipman Harrington, that hard, young disciplinarian, who had so often grumbled at them and whom they had so often silently cursed. Their rough hands were strangely gentle as they laid him in the litter they had made.

*   *   *

A naval chaplain conducted the funeral of the young officer. In the church at Hythe, near where Harrington had been stationed, he spoke in a sad, singing voice about a life of promise being pathetically cut off before it had flourished in the service of his country.

At the graveside he declared in echoing tones that something must be done to prevent a return to the days when gangs of smugglers terrorized the countryside.

Naval officers and ratings were joined at the funeral by revenue men and riding officers—and many a grocer, baker and innkeeper who had gratefully accepted an ancker of brandy if they had not actually taken part in secret nocturnal activities on the beach.

One of those present to hear the chaplain's words was Ransome Quested. He was, of course, greatly concerned in the matter. For did he not patrol the coast in this area, they said, and was he not himself a target for smugglers' guns?

When the service was over he walked alone to the inn near the church where he had left his horse. But he did not at once mount and ride. He took a seat in a secluded corner of the parlour and had a tankard of ale set before him.

As he drank he gave the events of the past days careful thought. Something, he decided, must be done about those events.

For a long time he stared at the dull pewter of the tankard on the polished oak table before him. Then, leaving the ale half-drunk, he rose and strode from the inn. Mounting, he took the road for Folkestone, where the chief customs officer for the district had his office.

He found that gentleman, a portly, short-sighted individual of the name of Fordingham, bending closely to the papers on his desk as though he were grovelling in them. He straightened in his chair as the visitor was shown in.

"Ah," he said, absent-mindedly, "if it isn't Mr.——"

"Ransome Quested, riding officer."

"To be sure, Mr. Quested, to be sure. And what brings you here, eh?"

"I came, Mr. Customer Fordingham, with my diary of patrols."

"Ah, but you did not require to see me about the matter. You could have left your diary in the outer office, as is usual."

"I have already left it there. But you see, Mr. Customer, that was only one reason for my visit."

"You wished to speak to me—about some other matter, Mr. Quested?"

"I did—and one of some urgency, I fear."

"And what, Mr. Quested, might that be?"

"The matter of Mr. Midshipman Harrington."

"Ah, yes. A dreadful affair."

"An outrageous one, sir."

"As you say, an outrageous affair. But I fear further talk on the matter will not mend it. The poor Midshipman is dead, and we cannot bring him back to life."

"I did not come here to attempt such a miracle, sir. I came to discuss, with your permission, the return of murdering gangs on our shore."

With an irritable gesture, Fordingham took snuff from a silver box on his desk and snapped the lid shut. He had received preferment to his present post entirely because of a family connection, and so long as the customs service in Kent ran itself then he was well pleased. Confound the fellow and his wish to discuss smugglers. "I would remind you, my good sir, that free trading on this coast has not been allowed to get out of hand for a considerable time."

"Until now."

"I do not quite understand you, sir."

"Then I will be explicit." The riding officer laid his hat on the desk and, without being invited to do so, drew up a chair and sat down. "It is true that for many years smugglers in these parts have gone about their business in a peaceable manner, bringing in a few casks here and a few there and quietly disposing of them. The preventive service which you run, sir, was strengthened and it did very well."

"Thank you." Fordingham was sufficiently gratified to offer his snuff.

"But then the war came. Most of the revenue cutters had to return to their original function and sail as naval vessels. I for one saw possibilities in this new state of affairs. I saw that the free traders could take advantage of the position.

"I visualized a return to the highly organized gangs, who might once again conduct their activities on a larger scale. I feared they might terrorize the countryside. I think the murder of Midshipman Harrington is an example of what I had feared."

" 'Tis but an example," said Fordingham.

"But not the last—unless something be done."

Fordingham moved uncomfortably in his chair. "I am not so sure it is for us to move in this matter. Mr. Pitt has done so much to put down the smugglers. I am sure he will take note of the incident of which you speak."

"Mr. Pitt has other matters on his mind, and they are of some urgency."

"Agreed."

"Consequently, I am of the opinion, sir, that if anything is to be done we must do it ourselves."

"I do not follow your meaning."

"Well, sir, if Napoleon Bonaparte is to invade our shores the country must be united in its attempts to repel such an invasion. We want the smugglers to work *with* us in this matter, not *against* us."

"A moment, Mr. Quested. You are no doubt a good riding officer—I am sure that you are—but do you not think it possible that you are dabbling in aspects of the situation that are—er, not quite your responsibility? Or beyond your know-ledge? I might say I am well informed of the situation on the Kent and Sussex coasts. Did you know, for instance, that many of the smuggling craft have thrown in their lot with the look-out vessels and that some of the free traders are offering to fight on land if the French fleet do come?"

"I did. Moreover, I am one who has suggested it."

Fordingham leaned forward abruptly. "Indeed, sir. You

are a remarkable fellow. What did you suggest, may I ask?"

"I suggested to Lieutenant Hogan at the naval station at Dungeness that the smugglers of Dymchurch were willing to stand their ground if the French land near their village."

" 'Pon my word, sir, how did you know they were of such a mind?"

"I am a riding officer—or did you forget, sir?—and I'd say such a one should do more than patrol the coast. I'd say he should make it his business to know those he may suspect— and how their brains work."

"Praiseworthy, Mr. Quested. Most praiseworthy."

"Thank you, sir. In fact, it was the parson who hinted at the matter. Now *he's* a remarkable fellow, sir. I fancy he has their confidence—to some extent."

"You do more than many a riding officer would do."

"England at this moment is in danger—and I am an Englishman. That is why I concern myself with this murder. If it is left unchallenged the free traders will grow too confident. It would be the old days of the gangs again—and we do not want that, not while there's a war in progress."

"We do not."

"Then, as I have said, if anything is to be done we must do it ourselves, for the government is much occupied with the war. That is why I came, for I have a suggestion to make. Ask, I plead of you, for a Bow Street Runner to be brought in from London to investigate the murder."

"A Bow Street Runner?"

"Aye, a thieftaker. 'Tis not so remarkable. The customs authorities have requested the services of such gentlemen in the past. Ask for the loan of a Runner. It is within your authority. You can request the magistrate at Bow Street Police Office to send such a fellow and, as is usual, pay him so long as he is engaged on the case."

"An excellent idea." Fordingham rose ponderously, and his podgy hands were trembling with excitement. "I must keep my district in good order. Damme if I don't send to Bow Street this very day. My thanks to you, Mr. Quested. I am delighted to have such as you in my service."

Quested rose and reached for his hat. "Then if you are pleased with my suggestion, might I ask that you make a written record of it. One never knows, one day it may assist my preferment in the service."

The riding officer went on his way well pleased with his day's work, and the district customer, penning a letter at once to Sir Richard Ford, the chief magistrate at Bow Street, was equally gratified. For soon he would have a professional investigator prodding his long nose about his patch of coast and putting fear in the heart of every smuggler for miles.

CHAPTER FOUR

THE CHIEF CUSTOMS officer at Folkestone was not the fool he seemed on first acquaintance. He had done much squinting near to the paper and scrawling with a podgy hand, but the letter to the Bow Street Police Office was very much to the point, suggesting plainly that the incident at Madman's Cove was a threat to national security.

It brought yet another concern to the mind of Sir Richard Ford, the chief magistrate at that office and one-time Member of Parliament for East Grinstead. An ageing man, though only 45 years old, he wrestled with the almost impossible task of fighting crime in a city unequalled for it anywhere in the world.

For a personal salary of £400 a year, with another £300 in lieu of fees and emoluments, he was responsible for catching the sneak-thieves, footpads and murderers as well as trying and sentencing them. And to assist him in his work he had only four-score constables, armed with carbines and cutlasses, to patrol the streets.

But on his staff he had six able lieutenants—certain clever individuals who investigated crime. They were variously known as peace officers, thieftakers or Bow Street Runners.

As London's first detectives, their existence had been kept as secret as possible since their inception. But a former magistrate, Sir John Fielding, nicknamed The Blind Beak, had written a pamphlet entitled *An Account of the Rise and Establishment of the Real Thieftakers*. And now, despite the odium heaped on their profession by a police-hating public, the six officers were making quite a name for themselves.

Of these Sir Richard, being human, had one who was a favourite, a man of stature rather less than middle height and a bright, clean-shaven countenance. His name was Harry Adkins, an officer justly proud of the nickname he had earned— *The Little Ferret.*

Whenever Sir Richard had on his hands a problem which at first glance seemed insurmountable, it was him he sent for, and it was him he called for now.

The magistrate invited Adkins to take a seat and handed him the letter from Fordingham to read. "What," he asked, do you think of that, Mr. Adkins?"

"I do not know enough about it as yet to think anything about it," the officer replied when he had read it. "I reserve my judgment, your honour."

"An excellent reply," said the magistrate. "But does the idea of a trip to Kent intrigue you, eh? Would you like to prod your sensitive nose into the affair so that in time you may risk a calculation on the matter?"

"I think a whiff of sea air might considerably aid my constitution," said Adkins, smiling broadly. "Indeed, sir, I feel I could become most interested in attempting to find the person or persons who would murder an officer of His Majesty's Navy at a time like this. When would you like me to set off?"

"Now, Mr. Adkins—before any more meet the same fate as Mr. Midshipman Harrington."

"Very good, sir," said the detective, rising. "Consider I am on my way."

"If you would wait a few minutes," suggested Sir Richard, reaching for pen and paper, "you may deliver my reply to Mr. Customer Fordingham in person."

The note he gave to Adkins read :

Bow Street Public Office,
Covent Garden,
London.

John B. Fordingham, Esq.,
The Customs House,
Folkestone,
Kent.

Dear Sir,

The bearer of this letter, Harry Adkins, Esquire, is the officer I am sending to you to investigate the foul murder of which you have notified me. He is a thieftaker of the highest integrity, and I trust he will accomplish his task in a manner satisfactory to the common good of the country, for I am appreciative of the implications involved, and to yourself in the particular.

You may retain his services so long as you require them for this specific case, and whilst engaged on it he will be entitled to a payment from you of a guinea per day and also fourteen shillings each day to cover his expenses.

Yours faithfully,
Richard Ford,
Chief Magistrate.

Placing the letter in a pocket of his dark, long-tailed jacket, Adkins paused at the doorway of the magistrate's room. "I take it the public coach might be overlong in setting me down on the Kentish coast, your honour?"

"In this case, much too long, Mr. Adkins."

"Then with your permission, sir, might I be driven down by one of the fast curricles used on occasions by this office? I am not, I venture to suggest, the best horseman in England."

"From what I hear, not by any means, Mr. Adkins," remarked Sir Richard, smiling as at some private memory. "But you *are* one of the best thieftakers. Certainly you may take a curricle, but order the driver to return with it as soon as he has deposited you in Kent."

"Thank you, sir. 'Twill make my task the easier."

The magistrate looked up from his desk, and a frown cancelled any sign of jocularity that had passed between the two. "I have a feeling that this case," he said, "will be far from easy."

*   *   *

Adkins went at once to his locker in the police office and took out a valise. Into this he put an assortment of wigs and incredibly old clothes, together with materials that might have come from an actor's dressing-room.

But the clothes he was to wear for the journey were vastly different. Over his tight, pale pantaloons of nankeen—a style of breeches as yet only the most daring favoured—he drew a fashionable pair of Hessian boots. His satin waistcoat was of the best, and he exchanged his dark jacket for a long-tailed, well-tailored tan one of the mode. Into a pocket of this he transferred the letter and a notebook.

On the inside of his locker he had a long mirror fixed, for vanity was not missing from his character, and he believed that a smart appearance brought respect from many whom he interviewed. So peering into the mirror with a satisfied smile, he gave a last tweak to his neckwear and patted his new, tall and pale-coloured top-hat into place on his head. Then he threw a high-collared, frogged greatcoat over his arm, picked up his silver-knobbed, polished cane and the bag and stepped jauntily out into Bow Street.

Harry Adkins was quite a dandy, and on this bright, spring day he could afford to wear his best. With a guinea paid to him every week by the magistrate and profitable assignments like this to be picked up, he decided that his was a profession of the most respectable.

Seating himself in the curricle, the thieftaker ordered his driver to take him first to a shop near Covent Garden. In this he bought a heavy, navy blue jersey, a pair of thick trousers, a seaman's jacket and a knitted woollen cap.

Climbing again to his perch on the curricle, he clapped the driver on the shoulder. "Right, me boy-o," he said, breezily, "off for the Kentish coast, and stop just before you drive this buggy into the sea."

Out of London they overtook the Folkestone Flyer, exchanging waves with the top-seat passengers as they bowled past it with grins on their faces.

The detective, determined to enjoy the drive, began to give forth in a mock falsetto, mouthing the words of a ditty of questionable merit. He thought to entertain his driver as well as himself. It was a mistaken belief. For singing, which he could never execute in tune, was not one of his better accomlishments.

> *I met a maid in Folkestone town* (he sang)
> *Who came upstairs and brought me down.*
> *She came to ask for a candle light*
> *To make her life as bright as bright.*
> *But off to bed with her I went,*
> *Off to hey-diddle-diddle I went.*

His companion made a wry face and joined him with gusto in the next verse, putting him on the right key and dissolving into laughter.

It was in these high spirits that the two drove at last into Folkestone. The journey had taken most of the day, but this was considered good time. On some stretches the road surface had been improved by a system suggested by two Scottish engineers, McAdam and Telford, of laying pieces of granite, and in the flying curricle they had at times reached speeds of 12 to 14 miles an hour.

But they had had to stop at turnpikes. They had also halted twice for tankards of ale, and once for a meal of pigeon pie, ham, cold beef, kidneys, steak, muffins and cheese. Harry Adkins lived well, knowing to his abiding satisfaction that his expenses would never be questioned.

"I fear it is too late to call upon the gentleman I have come

to see," remarked the thieftaker. "I do not think he will still
be at his desk. It is also too late for you to return to London
today. Consequently, my good fellow, hail the next passer-by
and inquire as to the name of the best inn in town."

Assured that *The Oddfellows' Arms* claimed that distinc-
tion, Adkins entered, doffing his top-hat and calling for the
landlord.

"My name is Adkins, of London," he said, carefully omitting
to mention Bow Street. "I will take a room, if you please, and
I should be glad if you would arrange for my man to stay for
the night also."

The innkeeper goggled at the fashion in which the visitor
was dressed, for even in London only a few of the young bucks
as yet sported the latest. The landlord bowed. "We shall be
honoured, sir," he said, bending forward again. "Shall you
be staying long, sir?"

"A few days," said Adkins, carelessly. "Longer maybe if
the fine weather holds. They say it is the new fashion to spend
holidays at the seaside."

"It is, sir, since the Prince o' Wales built hisself a place at
Brighton. But Lord save us, sir, there be hardly a parasol to
be seen here these days. They're all afraid the French'll
come."

"If Prinny still goes to Brighton, I wager they'll all flock
after him," declared Adkins.

"Aye, sir, but not to Folkestone."

"Well, my good sir, if you place before me the best of food,
and if I feel the benefit of my stay here, then I shall recom-
mend the place to my friends." Adkins was in an expansive
mood.

"You shall have a meal fit for a king."

"See to it, then, for I am ravenous."

In the parlour later Adkins engaged the landlord, who gave
his name as Barker, in conversation. "I trust there will be
certain diversions?" he began.

" 'Tis an interesting part o' the country, sir?"

"Didn't mean that. *Diversions*, man."

The landlord smiled wickedly. "Ah, meanin' the wenches—er, ladies, sir?"

"Didn't mean that exactly. But seeing you mention it, do I take it you could supply a wench—and no questions asked?"

The innkeeper winked slyly. "It's been known, sir."

"I'd wager it has. I'll keep it in mind. Do you know, landlord, I'm beginning to think you're an interesting fellow. But for the time being, what I meant was is anything exciting going on in these parts, anything that might—er, excite my curiosity?" Adkins was a man who could never start his inquiries too soon.

"Well, the doctors is fair worried."

"Oh, why?"

"It's the whirligigousticon."

"The *what*?"

"The whirligigousticon. It's a sickness that has broken out here. Fair number 'as it hereabouts. You ain't never heard o' it?"

"I am happy to say—never."

"Well, people wot 'as it sweats and feels giddy——"

"Very sorry for 'em, I'm sure. But I am not inclined to listen to all the horrible symptoms. If I get drunk, damme if I wouldn't think I'd got it."

"All right. But tell you what, sir, I can give you something to keep sickness away. Half a pint of water with the second rind of alder stick steeped in it, to be taken one hour afore breakfast."

"Ugh! Rather have ale with my breakfast. When I asked if anything *exciting* was happening, I did not mean whirligig-what's-its-name. I meant—oh, I don't know—news of the Frenchies being chased in the Channel, a man running helter-skelter after his wife's lover with his pistol primed, casks of brandy delivered in the dark——"

"You ain't referring to——" The innkeeper paused, placed a finger to his lips and lowered his voice, "the fair traders."

"I might be. I notice you call the *free* traders the *fair* traders. Are you one who thinks they trade *fairly*?"

"Don't rightly know wot to say," declared Barker. "You 'as to be careful with strangers. If you be talkin' o' wot I thinks you are, they prefers to be known as the *fair* traders, but like as not folk just calls 'em 'the gentlemen'. It's a bit scarey down 'ere, sir, and queer and all."

Adkins raised his brandy glass to the light, examining the pale liquid. "Damme, man, we're only having a conversation. What would you say, though, if I said I might be interested in *buying* some of this most excellent brandy?"

"Thought you was on holiday."

"So I am. So I am, landlord. But I do have one or two friends—er, in the same occupation as your good self. They might appreciate some of this—on the cheap."

"Try me again when I knows you better."

"Well said, sir. In the meantime, allow me to buy you a glass of your own brandy."

The landlord allowed several drinks to be pressed upon him, and Adkins watched his smile grow wider.

To himself the detective said: "What would I do without intoxicating liquor to help me in my work."

To the landlord he said: "Well, sir, do you think you know me better now?"

"I thinks you be of the most genial, sir."

"Splendid! A friendly fellow yourself, I'd say. Now what about a cask o' brandy to take home with me as—as a souvenir. But remember, I don't like paying over the odds for it."

The innkeeper raised his glass again and eyed the visitor over its rim. "You ain't by any chance——?"

"What ails you, man? We all like a bargain."

"You ain't—I mean, you ain't by any chance a riding officer or such like?"

"A riding officer? Pshaw! Peeping Toms, sir. Men who have nothing better to do. I do not care for the breed."

"Well, sir, if you will keep a silent tongue on it I'll introduce you to a certain party wot might be able to 'elp—I only says *might* be able to 'elp."

"Excellent." Adkins rose and looked through the sitting-room window. "Weather's blowing in from the sea," he observed. "Might have a storm before morning. Exciting things, storms, eh?"

"Aye, bloody nuisance as well. Can do some damage as well, they can."

"Speaking of excitement, does anything exciting ever happen around these parts?"

"You've not 'eard, then?"

"Not heard what?"

"Not 'eard o' the murder?"

"Indeed I have not. There has been a murder here?"

"That there 'as. A navy man. Midshipman. Shot dead 'e was."

"You don't say?"

"I do say. I says it most definite."

"Have they got he who did it?"

"No, they ain't—and never will neither. Not if I'm a judge o' the matter." Barker's voice fell almost to a whisper, as though even the shadows must not hear him. "Men as were near at the time—why, they don't know neither. Proper mystery it is."

"You do not mean to say, my good fellow, that no one knows *anything* about it?"

"Well, don't say as I says it—but the party wot might let you 'ave a cask o' you-know-what, reckon 'e knows as much as anybody, and that ain't much. But if I was you, sir, I'd be a bit careful o' gossiping about it. Reckon things is gettin' more'n dangerous around 'ere."

"Then can you take me to this—er, party?"

"Tomorrow—if you promises to be careful."

"Tomorrow it is then," said the detective, jovially. "Let us drink to it."

CHAPTER FIVE

THE LITTLE FERRET was at the customs house within minutes of its doors opening, for later that morning he had another and, he suspected, more important meeting than this with Mr. Customer Fordingham.

The clerk's eyes passed from the modish figure to the top-hat in one hand and the polished cane in the other and answered the visitor's greeting with nothing more than a quizzical raising of the eyebrows.

"Good morning," repeated Adkins, smiling blandly.

The clerk went so far as to nod, and the detective laid his hat and cane on the counter, denoting that he did not intend to leave immediately. "I should like to see Mr. Fordingham, please," he said.

"Name?" asked the clerk, in a tone indicative of his authority in the four square yards of the vestibule.

"Ah!" said the visitor, beaming and raising a gloved finger. "So you *do* have a tongue in your head. I am much relieved, for it makes things so much easier, don't you think? My name is Adkins."

"Where from?"

"London."

"Big place—London."

"Clever fellow, so it is. Nevertheless, that is where I am from."

"Whom do you represent?"

"Just tell Mr. Fordingham I am from London, if you will be so kind."

The clerk leaned back in his chair and scratched his head

with the top of his pen. Then he tried again. "What is your business with Mr. Fordingham?"

"Of that I shall enlighten him myself, when I see him. Just give him my name, if you please, and inform him I have come all the way from London to see him."

"Have you an appointment with Mr. Fordingham?" At last the clerk began to have an uncomfortable feeling that this ice-cool customer would win any battle of wits he cared to join.

"Shall we say that he may not be expecting to see me on this day and at this hour," supplied the thieftaker. "But he will not, I assure you, be surprised to see me. Please to tell him I am here, and if it is not inconvenient to you *without further delay*."

"*A gentleman from London.*" The words worked like magic on Fordingham, who never kept a visitor from the city waiting.

"Good day to you, sir," said the thieftaker, pausing until the clerk closed the door behind him. "Harry Adkins, of the Bow Street Police Office, at your service."

"Ah, Mr. Adkins, I am much relieved to see you," said the customs officer. "Take a seat, sir. Pray take a seat. So you are Sir Richard Ford's man, the gentleman he has sent to help me?"

"I have that honour," said the detective, handing over the letter the magistrate had penned.

"I am most pleased to see you, sir," said Fordingham. "Things have come to a pretty pass. The free traders have for long been going about their business in a more peaceable manner, and that God knows is bad enough. But now it would appear that the gangs are out again, and violence is breaking out once more."

"So I understand."

"You've heard about the poor midshipman, of course," expostulated Fordingham. "It's murder and no mistake. I'd hoped the tragedy might pull them up in their tracks. But not so, sir. Not so. Since I sent for you there has been yet another run and they marched through the high street of a town not a dozen miles away, bearing their stuff in the dark and with a veritable army about them clanking their cutlasses. As cheeky as you please. It is quite damnable."

The thieftaker's manner was calm and nonchalant, and the customs man, who had grown red in the face as he spoke, leaned back in his chair and brightened perceptibly. "However," he said, "when they know you are here it will take some wind out o' their sails."

"That," said Adkins, "is just the point. I would wish they do not know I am here."

But Mr. Adkins, that was my whole purpose in bringing you here—to frighten them by your presence."

"I should have thought," said the detective, "that mostly you would want to have the killer taken."

"Er, of course I do. I wish that also."

"Well, if I am to accomplish that task—why, sir, I must be allowed to do it in my own way."

"Why, certainly, Mr. Adkins."

"Then I ask that you do not tell anyone, not even your own clerk, any single thing about me save my name. I have, if I may say so, some long experience of criminal matters, and I find that if the guilty party knows I am a thieftaker too early in the proceedings he is put at once on his guard. Why, sir, he may even run away."

Fordingham's face was blank for a moment. "I shall do as you say," he said.

"Excellent. Now I must ask if any besides yourself knows I have been sent for?"

"Two persons only. Lieutenant Hogan, who is at Dungeness, and a riding officer, Ransome Quested by name, who also keeps shop at Dymchurch."

"Well, that is not too bad, sir, for we may presume that in their posts both may be men of character and discretion. I shall make it my business to have confidential talks with them both."

The thieftaker rose and took his hat and cane. "I shall call on you again from time to time, Mr. Fordingham. There will be the question of—er, my fees and expenses, and you may hear whispers that may be of value to me."

"I shall be most happy to assist you in any way."

"Thank you." Adkins paused, his hand on the door knob. "Oh, and by the way, do not be perturbed if I would seem to quite disappear. Sometimes it is best for it to appear I have vanished. When Sir Richard Ford, my superior at Bow Street, puts me on a case he does not expect to see me, or indeed hear from me, until my efforts have been fully rewarded."

Fordingham rose ponderously, the frown re-fixing itself on his forehead. "If you should vanish in these parts, and with all that is afoot," he said, solemnly, "I shall be bound to have some concern about it. I should be afraid that you would be found in a cliff cave or under a hedge—as dead as mutton."

"That, sir, is a risk I must take," returned the detective quickly. "But I do not think it is the greater for being here instead of London. Nevertheless, thank you for the warning."

*   *   *

Adkins returned to the *Oddfellows' Arms* and sought out Barker, the landlord, whom he found not so willing to help in daylight as he had been in candle-light.

"Off we go to see your brandy man," said the detective.

"Don't know as we ought," was the reply.

"Come, man, you promised."

"Aye, but that were yesterday. I've been thinking. When I've took a client along afore—well, there wasn't no murder then."

"Tut, man, if you think before every step you take you'll never go anywhere for a twelvemonth. Where does the gentleman live?"

"Not a dozen miles away."

"*Dymchurch?*"

"Aye. But 'arf a minute. How did you know that?"

"My mother was a witch, don't you know?" laughed Adkins. "No, my friend, I met a man this morning who told me I should visit Dymchurch. A quaint, old village, he said, and not a dozen miles away. I've a mind to ride over this minute, land-lord, whether you accompany me or not—and make inquiries as to who sells cheap brandy. If you fear for your skin, you stay home, my friend. But take it from me, this murder busi-ness is stuff and nonsense. I'll wager it was an accident and no murder at all."

" 'Appen you're wrong."

"Maybe. But you see before you a man innocent of any crime, and that will keep me safe."

" 'Appen it might."

"Come, man. Saddle a couple o' horses, and make mine a docile creature, for I'm an easy-going fellow, don't you know?"

There was no gainsaying that Harry Adkins, with his dandi-fied clothes, bland smile and comfortable, ambling gait, appeared of the most innocent and guileless—as many a crim-inal had thought until it was too late.

" 'Appen I'll go with you," said the innkeeper.

They took the cliff-path, and Adkins, who had been primed with the known details of the murder, kept a lookout for the windmill.

"What is that?" he asked when its gaunt outline appeared ahead.

"A windmill," said the innkeeper.

"Well, I never. A windmill. Let us take a closer look, for I'm fascinated by 'em."

"Don't go near it. That's where they did for 'im."

"My dear friend," smiled Adkins, "are you afraid of seeing his ghost?"

Barker had paled. " 'Taint only that," he said. "Yon' wind-mill 'as been 'aunted as long as I can remember."

"By Jehosaphat! But that interests me, Barker. I'm the son of a witch, don't you remember? *How* is it haunted?"

"It's well known round these parts." A wind was rising and its chill whipped Barker's cheeks paler still. "It's known as the devil dog or the phantom hound. A terrible animal it be, all white and lit up in the dark, and running mad round the windmill, and howling and making a fearful rattling noise. There ain't many comes 'ere after nightfall."

The wind rose higher, and Barker had to raise his voice to be heard above its wail. "Wouldn't come 'ere at night for a king's ransom, that I wouldn't. Midshipman's murder weren't the only one committed 'ere. Man wot built windmill did for someone inside it. 'Appened long ago, and they say the devil dog were his. Damn fool of a midshipman. Ought to 'ave known better'n come 'ere at night."

"Perhaps he did not know the tale."

" 'Appen 'e didn't."

"Or perhaps he came—er, in the line of duty."

"Fool," growled the innkeeper. " 'E should 'ave stayed away."

For a moment Adkins looked at his companion closely. "Strange that you should be so frightened of the ghost dog," he said, "with a name like yours."

"Wot d'yer mean?" asked the landlord, suspiciously.

"Bark—that's what a dog does, is it not? And your name is Barker."

The innkeeper sulked as they moved nearer to the track that led from the cliff-path to the windmill.

"Let us take a closer look," said Adkins, turning on to the track.

"Wouldn't if I was you, not after wot I was tellin' yer of."

"Nonsense, man. Ghosts do not walk in daylight."

"Don't go," said Barker.

"You stay then. I'm going."

Barker reined in his horse, but his curiosity apparently overcame his fears, for he then followed the thieftaker up the track. It was very lonely up near the windmill and a little eerie, even on this bright forenoon, with the old sails creaking overhead.

The catch of the door and one of its hinges were broken, and it was held in place by a large stone.

"Come on, my friend, help me to open it," said Adkins.

"Not on your life," said the innkeeper. "I ain't touching it."

Adkins rolled the stone away, hauled the door open and went inside. Barker followed him cautiously.

"Well, well, someone's not afraid of the place," observed the detective, picking up a hurricane lamp and examining the wick closely. "This has been lit quite recently."

The innkeeper watched silently as Adkins made a detailed inspection of the place, picking up in turn a rope, a length of twine, some pieces of tape and a miniature lantern that might have seemed more in place in a drawing-room.

Soon they were off again and riding before lunch into Dymchurch, where Barker made for a tavern named *The Ship*. Here he introduced Adkins to the landlord, a tall, brawny fellow of the name of Hackett.

"Staying at my place," explained Barker. "Down from Lunnon to get a breath o' sea air."

Adkins ordered brandy for all three, and when Hackett had gone to get it Barker put his mouth and a cupped hand to the thieftaker's ear. "That's 'im," he confided. "But ask 'im yerself."

Sipping the brandy later, Adkins said: "My dear Mr. Hackett, what excellent brandy. I do not think I have ever tasted the like—except at the house of Mr. Barker here."

"Aye," said Hackett, "same stuff, I shouldn't wonder."

"I did ask Mr. Barker if he'd let me buy a small cask of it, but he hadn't one to spare at the price I offered."

"What price was that?" asked Hackett.

"The price," said Adkins, lowering his voice and speaking very close to the man's ear, "of *moonshine*."

"Hey!" gasped the man. "What's this? Who *are* you?"

"Adkins is the name." The detective's smile was bland and innocent. "Had you forgotten?"

"I don't know who you are, Mr. Adkins, but I'd have you know I'm a respectable gent."

"Not a more respectable man on this 'ere coast," put in Barker. "Why, he sings in Parson Honeycombe's choir."

"I'd say Mr. Hackett looks *most* respectable. Didn't say otherwise, did I?" said Adkins, asking to be directed to the lavatory and leaving the two exchanging silent glances.

"Who the hell is he?" demanded Hackett as soon as the thieftaker had left the room.

"A London fop, I'd say," suggested Barker. "Bit of a fool, too. All smarmified, and mustn't 'ave an 'orse wot might gallop. Bet 'e piddles down 'is leg out there if 'e ain't careful."

Adkins returned and ordered more brandy. "About moonshine," he said.

"Keep your voice down," said Hackett.

"About moonshine," repeated Adkins, lowering his voice. "Is there much fair trading hereabouts?"

"Allus will be."

"Yes, indeed. But I hear the gangs are out again. Is there one in these parts?"

"Don't ask us, for we be respectable gents. But we do hear tales. They say there's a gang not a long way from 'ere."

"Well I never. Deuced exciting, eh? Can't wait till you tell me more." Adkins was rubbing his hands. "Who runs the gang? Could you name the leader? I say, maybe he could let me have a tub, just for my personal use, just for the hell o' it. Dammit, I've the money to pay."

"There's a boss o' the gang," said Hackett. "Well, there's got to be, ain't there?"

"Know who he is?" Adkins sprawled back in his chair, yawning a little, smiling guilelessly and dabbing his lips daintily with a lace-edged handkerchief.

"Well now, sir, that's a good question," said Hackett. "A very good question, ain't it, Barker? The gang has wot you might call a leader, they do say, and there's many a one knows who *he* is. But the real boss—well, they do say 'e keeps tucked right away out o' sight, and no one on God's blasted earth knows who he is. Why, mister, they do say that not one o' the gang knows his name—or what he looks like."

CHAPTER SIX

LANDLORD HACKETT, of *The Ship*, paused as he served the next round of drinks. " 'Ere," he said, his eyes narrowing, "wot d'yer want to know 'bout free traders' boss fer?" He was aware suddenly of the thought.

The Little Ferret blinked innocently over the rim of his raised glass. "Why, my good sir, is it not obvious? If I made his acquaintance—hey presto, I might have a source for my favourite brandy. You never do know, sir, he might take a liking to me."

"Well, if them as works for 'im ain't ever seen 'is face— well, sir, I'd say it's a 'undred to one a stranger the likes o' you 'ud never find out," grumbled Hackett.

"Then I will have to rely on the likes o' you," returned Adkins with a wink.

"Wot fer?"

"For a nice little ancker o' brandy, and no questions asked."

"All right, come and see me again," said Hackett. "If I gets to know you better, I might let you have a tub. But don't go talkin' about moonshine again. It makes me nervous."

The detective leaned back in his chair. "Came by an old windmill," he drawled, casually. "Most exciting. Mr. Barker tells me there was a murder there, and not ten days ago."

Hackett looked up suddenly, spilling his drink, and Adkins fancied there was a paleness beneath the crust of tan on his face. Hackett, it would appear, did not spend all his days shut up in his tavern.

"Wot wus you telling 'im?" Hackett treated Barker to a long glare.

"I wus tellin' 'im about the midshipman."

"Oh."

The detective leaned forward. "Most exciting, is it not? Never thought a spin down here would provide such a diversion. Has the guilty party been taken?"

"Been taken?" echoed their host. "Not on your life, sir. There ain't no one wot knows who done it—'cepting he who did."

"Well, I never," exclaimed Adkins. "What a place I've chosen to take the air. Smuggling. Murder. Are the two connected, d'you think?"

"They say as that could be so," put in Barker, enthusiastically. "There was a run——"

"Joseph Barker!" Hackett cut in before the Folkestone innkeeper could finish his words. "Surprised at you I am. Tittletattling with strangers. You see, sir, we're one 'appy family hereabouts, and a bit close with strangers, if you see what I mean. Now, now, Joseph Barker, don't bring your Folkestone ways to Dymchurch."

"Don't be hard on the fellow," laughed Adkins. "Only showing me round he was. Fascinated with windmills I am— and asked Mr. Barker all about it as we passed by. Strange goings on there at night, so they say."

"*Wot* strange goings on?" Hackett's voice was tense.

Adkins put his thumbs to his cheeks, moved his fingers up and down, and leered comically. "Ghosts!" he said in mockserious tones.

"Shouldn't take it so light, if I wus you. That place is 'aunted right enough."

"Fiddlesticks! I'm not scared. I'll tell you this, my good fellow, I'm afraid of a pistol or a carbine popping off within a good quarter mile of me. But I fear no ghost, let it caper a few feet away. Tell you what, Mr. Landlord, sir—I'll visit the windmill at midnight tonight. Care to accompany me, eh?"

"Don't go," said Hackett.

"Why not?"

"Just don't. I'm warnin' yer, don't go."

" 'Twould be fun to make the acquaintance of a ghost, don't you think? No, I won't take your warning. I promise you I shall go—and this night."

"Wouldn't go with you for a 'undred in gold guineas," declared the Folkestone landlord. "That I wouldn't."

"Nor me neither," said the Dymchurch man, scowling darkly. "And don't forget, I'm warning yer——"

"Then I shall go myself, sirs, and be damned to you. Mr. Barker, pray have a stiff brandy and some hot soup ready against my return tonight."

The two visitors from Folkestone rose to go. At the door the detective placed a hand on the shoulder of the Dymchurch landlord and a mouth close to his ear. "Don't forget the tub," he said, in a low voice, "and not a word to a soul."

"If you be alive to drink it." Hackett stood grim-faced in the tavern doorway, watching them mount and ride, and when they had gone he threw a cloak over his apron and hurried down the high street and into a narrow alley. In minutes he was rapping on the door of a cottage, gabbling urgently to the man who opened the door.

"Get an 'orse this minute," he said, "and ride to Bart Barley with a message. . . ."

*   *   *

The village was scarcely out of sight behind the two horsemen when an incident occurred that was to have a profound effect on the detective's thoughts.

A beautiful bay came towards them from the opposite direction, high-stepping and throwing its head. They could see at once that the animal was a thoroughbred and of a nervous disposition. The figure on it, mounted side-saddle, appeared to be having some difficulty in controlling it, and when they were yet several hundred yards away a dog darted from a clump of trees and set up a sudden barking at the horse's hind legs.

At once the high-spirited animal bolted, and its rider, white-faced beneath her plumed riding hat, clung helplessly as it thundered towards them.

Before it was upon them Adkins had wheeled his horse and had it quickening speed in the same direction, urging it to the gallop as the maddened animal was overtaking his own mount. The two horses moved abreast of each other for some distance, Adkins edging in towards it, and finally he had a tight hold on the bridle of the runaway, bringing it gradually to a halt.

Its frightened rider leaned over on to Adkins's shoulder, and he became aware of a delightful contact with a young woman of little more than one and twenty. Her hat and crop gone, her red-gold hair blew in his face and he was conscious of a perfume that was not of the country lane.

He put an arm about her shoulders to steady her, and soon she was able to speak. "I—I am most grateful, sir. But for your intervention I must have been—sorely hurt." She was breathing deeply, but he thought her voice the most fascinating he had ever heard.

He was not fully aware of her actual words, for he was studying her closely and deciding that her appearance was quite utterly delightful.

Under much patting and coaxing the horse quietened, and Adkins then raised his top-hat. "Ma'am," he said, smiling, and the practised interviewer could not understand why he was so short of words.

The innkeeper rode up with her hat and crop, and she forced a smile as she took them.

"Thank you, sir," she said to the detective. "I cannot thank you enough——"

"It is my pleasure, ma'am. Pleased to be of service. Perhaps you would allow me to escort you on your way, in case that animal makes off again?"

"It would be most kind of you, sir. I admit I am a little startled, and you would have but a mile to go out of your way.

I live at the vicarage at Dymchurch, where my father has the living of the parish."

As the two men fell in beside her, making back in the direction from which they had come, and keeping a watchful eye for any further sign of restiveness in the young woman's horse, she patted the creature.

" 'Tis a beautiful beast, ma'am," said Adkins, admiringly, "if a little dangerous."

"Yes, my father bought him for me," she explained, "and he would not appear to be yet sufficiently used to me."

"If I may say so, your father must have paid highly for him." The thought crossed Adkins's mind that a country vicar would not in normal circumstances be able to buy such a handsome animal.

"You'll be Miss Honeycombe, then, milady?" said the innkeeper.

"I am, sir. I am Susannah Honeycombe."

At the vicarage the young lady insisted on presenting the two to her father, so that he may add his thanks to her own.

The stalwart vicar of St. Peter's and St. Paul's, whom Adkins thought more like the rumbustious captain of a privateer than a Clerk in Holy Orders, poured wine in glasses of the finest crystal.

"Now you, sir," said Honeycombe, handing one to Barker, "I have seen you before, have I not? Folkestone, that is it. The *Oddfellows' Arms*, eh? But you, sir, you are a stranger in these parts, are you not?"

"I am," said the man from Bow Street. "I am from London."

"Here on some—er, business?"

"Taking the air, vicar. Taking the air. The seaside resorts have become quite fashionable, don't you know, since the prince built his pavilion at Brighton——"

"Just so. And you are staying at the *Oddfellows' Arms* at Folkestone?"

"I am—for the present, and I do admit to feeling better already, for what diversions have been laid before me since I came!"

"Ah," said the vicar.

"I have just, if I may say so, Miss Honeycombe, had the honour of rescuing a lady in distress, and tonight on the stroke of midnight I am to visit a windmill where a murder took place but recently and which is reputed to be haunted."

The vicar towered over the detective, looking down at him strangely. "Which windmill, might I ask, is arousing your interest?"

"That at Madman's Cove," supplied Barker. "But don't look at me, vicar, I ain't a-going."

"I should think not. It is true that a most unfortunate murder took place there a week ago or more, but why dwell on it, sir?"

"Just want to see if the place is haunted," said Adkins, smiling. "Haunted! No more than a countryman's fancy, I'll be bound."

"I should not be so sure." Vicar Honeycombe's voice was low, but it contained a vibrant note.

"Surely you do not—I mean haven't you been down to the windmill?"

"Yes, but—er, only by daylight. I have never been near it after dark."

"You are not afraid, you a man of the Church?"

"I do not pander to such tales. But if I were you, sir, I would not go to that windmill tonight."

The detective flashed the most genial of smiles. "Why ever not, vicar?"

"I do not think it would be good for your health." There was a grim set to the cleric's mouth and chin.

"Nonsense, vicar. I cannot think of a more entertaining holiday spree."

"Very well, do not take my warning, then. But allow me to say that there are they who have passed by that spot at night who would not again go within two miles of it after nightfall. And some of them have never been the same again. . . ."

Later, bidding Adkins farewell, the vicar said: "Heed my warning, sir. You would not seem a big, nor yet a robust enough man to survive what may befall you there."

CHAPTER SEVEN

BACK IN FOLKESTONE the Bow Street Runner left the landlord before they reached the inn, saying he wished to wander about the town and acquaint himself the better with it. Instead he paid another call at the customs office.

"I have a favour to ask of you," he said to Fordingham. "Can you let me have a key to your office? I am setting out this evening on an—er, expedition. I would wish to change my clothes before doing so, and I would not particularly wish they at the *Oddfellows' Arms* to see me in another character."

"I will offer you greater hospitality than that, Mr. Adkins," said the customs man. "You may come to my house for that purpose. I will tell you directly where to find it, and you may visit me there any time you wish. What time may I expect you?"

"It is most kind of you. Shall we say eight of the clock?"

"A good time, Mr. Adkins, for then you may dine with me before setting out to wherever you wish to go."

"Thank you. I shall look forward to that."

"Excellent—and if I might know where you are going I might be able to give you even more assistance."

"I intend to explore the area where the murder took place—and I propose to do so in the dark."

"Then I can arrange for someone to accompany you—a riding officer say—to guard your person. It would not now seem a place to visit alone—and especially after nightfall."

"Thank you, but I would wish to go alone."

"As you wish, Mr. Adkins. As you wish. No doubt you know your own job best. Then I shall see you at eight?"

"Yes." On the point of leaving, the thieftaker paused for a moment longer. "What do you know," he asked, "of Parson Honeycombe, the vicar of Dymchurch?"

"Parson Honeycombe? I do not know the man well, and they say no one does. Why do you ask?"

"Just that I met him today and I thought him an unlikely fellow for a cleric."

Fordingham pursed his lips. "I have heard it said that he is reckoned to be a good preacher, and that in his parish he is well liked—and feared, too. I am afraid that is all I can tell you about him."

Jogging down the high street, Adkins thought he would have liked to inquire also about that preacher's daughter. Such questions, however, could wait—though he had to admit that the person of Susannah Honeycombe and her face and her smile had that afternoon occupied a trifle more of his thoughts than might have seemed necessary. Her the daughter of a raw-boned, weather-beaten giant of a man? It did not seem somehow quite in keeping. . . .

At the *Oddfellows' Arms* he took his saddle-bag to his room, and into it stuffed the woollen cap, seaman's jersey and coarse, thick trousers he had brought with him.

In the yard he hung the bag at the saddle bow and rode off, still top-hatted and tailed.

He found Fordingham's house without much difficulty. It lay outside the town, secluded in tree-clad grounds, with stables and out-buildings some distance from the house. Adkins noted these latter and asked that he may leave the suit he would take off in one of the out-houses as he did not expect to return until long after midnight.

"By all means." Fordingham led to one of the out-buildings. It had a heavy oak door and a small, high window protected by iron bars. From the outside it resembled a small prison, but inside were a small bed, a table and two wooden chairs, and the walls were cleanly white-washed.

"It was once a groom's bedroom," explained the detective's

host. "It has a key which you may keep always in your pocket, and you may use the place as often as you please."

"It could be most useful," mused Adkins. "I will take you up on the offer."

"Then it is yours so long as you stay in these parts," said Fordingham with a genial smile.

The moon had risen by the time the customs man's guest, dressed for scrambling over rocks and exploring cliff-paths, led his horse quietly from the stable and set off down the coast road. No one would have taken him for the immaculate little London fop, nor did he wish on this night to be recognized as such.

When the time came for his true identity and his mission to be revealed, he decided, he might allow it to be widely known that he was making a lonely trip to Madman's Cove and see what happened then. But not tonight.

Certainly no one would have recognised him as he rode the rolling downs, for sinister clouds had drifted in like a dark continent roofing the world.

Without the moon for company, he passed through Hythe, neither hurrying nor dawdling, and any who were out of doors did not give him a second glance.

When he took the cliff-path that led to the cove he strained his eyes for the windmill on the skyline, and when it came into view he approached it warily, looking for somewhere to leave his horse so that he could approach it on foot. He found a copse and tethered the animal to a tree.

On the path again, he paused for a moment, gazing at the windmill on its hump-backed hill. Seen at night-time, it was black and forlorn, like a dark, sub-human figure with strange, ragged arms drooping in despair.

In the evil dark which bred the spirits of the night there was indeed something strange about this mill where no man lived or worked. The little thieftaker, for all his shrewdness, was no superhuman being, possessing as he did all the nervous fears to which his kind were heir—and a few of his own imaginative ones besides. This was not the kind of assignment he liked. But in apparent contradiction it was the sort he did best. He shuddered as though an ice-cold gust whistled in from the sea.

He did not go at once to the windmill, for it was not yet midnight, and he planned first to explore Madman's Cove below it at the time of night when the young midshipman had met his death. He did not know what he was looking for, but he thought it a reasonable idea.

At the spot where Mr. Midshipman Harrington's men had challenged the smugglers, the thieftaker looked down into the cove. In the moonless dark there were vague shadows, but they were as still as primeval rock; the ceaseless sound of wind and tide rose and fell, as though beating time to some great, sad work of music long ago and for ever dead. Incessantly the sea washed and smoothed, and it seemed that no man had ever ventured down to its frothing, licking tongue—and would not ever do so.

Harry Adkins, who was more at home in the darkest London alley, shuddered again.

Then he picked his way carefully down the winding, twisting path. Gaining the beach, he scrunched through pebbles and scuffed through sand until he was far out near the sea. Turning, he studied the cliffs. The path he had taken seemed to be the only way down, and apart from it there were only sheer dark lines that looked like narrow fissures in the earth and rock.

Suddenly two points of light appeared on the cliff top and began to follow the course of the path down towards the beach.

Adkins dropped to the wet sand and lay on his belly, his head raised to watch. He was glad he was not wearing his elegant best.

The lights, he decided, must be lanterns, for they swung from side to side, and at times went out as though they vanished for a moment behind a boulder that screened them from view.

The two lights reached the bottom of the path and moved along under the cliff for a time until, one after the other, they disappeared. The point where this had occurred was where a dark line in the cliff face indicated what might be a cleft.

Adkins rose carefully to his feet, not taking his eyes from the spot, and began to walk towards it. When he reached it he found it to be nothing more than a narrow fissure, but he moved into it and after a few yards found the narrow passage widening. He became aware of a glow of light beyond.

Cautiously he took a few more steps. Then he flattened himself against the stone wall. Just ahead the passage widened out unexpectedly into a cave.

Two lanterns rested on rock ledges, and a dozen men sat on their haunches beside a number of barrels and boxes. Adkins had found the hiding place where the smugglers kept some of the contraband if they did not bring enough carts to take it all away when the vessel came. The men had opened one of the casks, and were drinking from tin mugs. Their voices echoed back to the detective. . . .

"Knows 'ow to make this stuff over there, that they do."

"Over where? Come on man, speak yer bloody mind. No one can 'ear yer. France yer mean, doncher?"

"I do and all. God bless bloody France and 'er brandy."

There was a short silence. Then conversation broke out again.

"Wot about 'im wot got shot dead?"

"The bastard blockader, yer mean?"

"Aye."

"Well, wot about 'im?"

" 'Oo did for 'im?"

" 'Oo cares?"

"I was just thinkin'——"

"Thinks too bloody much yer does. Nobody knows 'oo did fer 'im."

"Queer though."

"Queer?"

"Aye, Bart went over to windmill just afore it 'appened."

"Bart'd skin yer alive if 'e 'eard yer sayin' that."

"Bart ain't 'ere, and Bart ain't 'eard me say it, and if yer tells 'im I'll kick yer in the bleedin' cods."

"All right, I'll not tell 'im. But we can't stay 'ere argufyin' all night. Nor drinkin' neither. We've to get some o' the casks out o' 'ere tonight. Come on, mates, show a leg there. And 'ide them mugs and the tub wot we've opened."

The detective moved carefully back through the passage, walked a short distance under the shadow of the cliffs away from the foot of the path and hid behind a boulder.

Soon the men appeared carrying casks, and struggled to the clip top, their lanterns twisting upwards like huge glow-worms. They returned for one more load. Then came the sound of trundling carts from above, dying away on the night air.

Adkins then re-entered the cave and explored it as best he could without the aid of a lantern. He found it partly open to the sky, and groping around found a number of casks and boxes remaining. Obviously this was one of the gang's secret storehouses, to which they returned from time to time.

He left the beach, gaining the downs above and finding no sign of life. He began to trudge towards the windmill.

The clouds had thinned and the night was lighter now, though the moon still hid its face. The paler the night the starker the outlines of the lonely tower, the more visible its old walls which had once been white-washed, but were now grey like some indeterminate and gigantic ghost. He was not far off now. The wind moaned about the rotting sails, making them protest eerily.

Who would come to the old mill alone on a night like this, specially with the tales they told of it? The solitary figure paused, wishing for a moment that he had accepted Fordingham's offer of company in the person of a riding officer. But the Little Ferret did like to work alone.

There was a gust of wind louder than the rest. The mill door swung open. There was a howl stranger than any wind. And from the darkness within something hurtled, a leaping, cavorting thing, pale and shapeless in the dark and topped by a flickering light like a jack o' lantern.

Adkins, who had moved forward again, halted. He stood very still. Soon he could make out the form of a dog. The Phantom Hound. *The Thing* of local legend.

For any law-abiding villager of Dymchurch that would have been enough. But not for Harry Adkins and his inquiring mind. For one thing he had half-expected something like this. For another the yelping of *The Thing* was distinctly more canine than ghostly. But the Bow Street Runner went on and up.

The animal raced away, the light on its back suddenly going out.

For an instant the detective paused at the open door. Then he went in.

"Be you Mr. Adkins, sir?" said a voice from the darkness. "Mr. Adkins from Lunnon?"

"Who are you?" asked the thieftaker. "Pray show yourself, or I will drag you outside and see for myself."

" 'Old back, Mr. Adkins. Not so bold, sir, and do not step forward. Stay in the doorway where there's light to see you. One o' my friends is at yer back, with a pistol pointin' at yer arse."

Someone must have come from behind the windmill, for Adkins could feel the muzzle of the weapon jabbing into his back.

"What is the meaning of this?" he barked, summoning as much dignity as he could into his voice.

"It means we wus expecting you," said another voice from behind.

The owner of the voice inside the mill moved forward a little, but did not come into the light. "We've a message for you, Little Mister Meddler, and we'll knock it inter yer thick skull. Go back to Lunnon directly, and stick to yer own business, leavin' the fair trade to them as knows it. Right, Jedd, knock it in——"

The voice went on speaking, but Adkins heard no more. For he was struck on the head from behind with some blunt and heavy weapon, and he crumpled to the ground and lay still.

CHAPTER EIGHT

HE WHO CALLED himself Adams was on the way to his fortnightly assignation with the man who came from London, and who was in the habit of meeting him at Maidstone, which was roughly halfway.

Dressed in a caped, high-collared overcoat, knee-breeches, a broad-brimmed, low-crowned hat and a black cravat of the finest, and driving himself in a two-horse chaise, Adams might have given the appearance of a country squire, though his great weight and height and his weathered features suggested more the successful farmer.

He did not take the coach, or it would have cost him all of fifteen shillings for an inside place, with an extra eight-and-sixpence if he took luggage. And Mr. Adams was a man with a mania for collecting money, of which he now had not an inconsiderable amount, rather than spending it.

Besides the open chaise gave this withdrawn and solitary-seeming man an excuse to wear a concealing muffler as against the wind.

At Maidstone he drove into the yard of the *Royal Star*, which was their meeting place, but finding that the London coach had not yet arrived took a seat in the bar parlour, waiting for the man he was to meet to order and pay for a private room rather than himself.

When he heard the coach-horn and a bustle in the yard he went out and waited for the travellers to alight from the stage. Last to step down was a gentleman wearing a long, dark, full-skirted greatcoat and black top-hat and carrying an ebony, silver-knobbed cane in a grey-gloved hand. He had a pale, smooth-skinned countenance on which very black eyebrows contrasted rather oddly, and his grave expression was as sober as his clothes.

His name, as far as anyone in England was concerned, was John Henry Manners.

He looked about him quickly, and seeing Adams strode swiftly over to him. "Ah, my friend," he said, "you are in good time."

The two went into the inn where, waiting to be shown to a private room, they chatted about the affairs of the day, the newcomer doing most of the talking, in voluble English that some might have thought a trifle too precise.

"Do you know, sir, that there is an outbreak of the small-pox in town? You did not? Did you know, then, that there is now an antidote? It is called vaccination. The surgeons have been using the method for some time and find it most satis-factory."

"I must acquaint you of a new marvel of the age. One of the London companies is entirely heating its offices with *gas*— and some of the employees, thinking the flame went all down the pipe, spent most of the day feeling them to see if they were becoming too hot."

But the moment the door of the private room was locked behind them, the man from London underwent a remark-able change. His practised smile vanished and his mouth set in a hard line. He was stiff-backed and vital, strutting to a table and laying down his cane as it were a sword. And his questions were abrupt, like precise military orders.

"You have something for me?" he asked. "A letter perhaps?"

Adams's reply was to draw from a pocket a crumpled enve-lope bearing no name and address, and this he handed over as the two sat down at the table.

"I am glad you do not fail me," was all the thanks Man-ners gave. "Now please to answer my questions."

"There is one reason why I do not fail you," said Adams,

through lips set as hard as those of his companion, "and that is the money you pay."

"Ah, money! It is a useful commodity. What remarkable tricks it can make people play. 'Tis the most important tool of my trade—and of many others, eh?"

" 'Tis the only reason why I serve you—do not forget it," declared Adams.

"Quite so. Now listen carefully—do you bring me any intelligence by word of mouth?"

"Only that the port of Roscoff is now to the satisfaction of your—er, correspondent there."

"It will attract the English—I mean our smugglers then?"

"It is a port that will not be neglected by *me*. I cannot speak for others."

"So—the port of Roscoff will do good business in English gold guineas and intelligence?"

"How many free traders will deal in intelligence as well as gold I do not know. *I* have the stomach for it. You must thank God for that."

"Pray not so touchy, Adams, my friend——"

Adams's fist crashed down on the table and there was a ferocious glare in his eyes. "I have warned you before, do not refer to me by that or any other name. It may slip from your tongue when there are ears to listen."

"Contain yourself, man. I do not care for table-thumping. Besides, it cannot be your real name—or you're the biggest fool in Christendom."

"It is the name by which some of my associates know me. That is enough to make it dangerous. Now to talk of other things. I refer to a matter of money. To be precise—the payment you promised for this most recent favour. My fee, sir. I shall be happy to take possession of it without further delay."

The face of the man from London was expressionless. "I am sorry," he said, "but I do not have it."

"You do not have it?" Adams flared. "Can it be that you

do not understand? I do not play dangerous games for nothing."

"Precisely. But I await more funds from France. Until I get them——"

"In the name of God, man, do you not know what I have risked for you?"

"I have paid you in the past, and I will pay you in the future—in full. Pray do not let us have any nonsense. I am quite well aware of what your service entails." Manners was forcing a smile.

"I do not think so. I would have you know, for instance, that in connection with your affairs a certain midshipman has got himself shot."

"Shot?"

"Murdered, sir! *Murdered!* That might be a more accurate term."

Manners's smile vanished, leaving his face graver than before. "How did this happen? Someone has been clumsy, eh?"

"Clumsy or not—it had to be. The fellow would have had your letter else. *Your* affairs were responsible, not mine."

"Yours, too, had you been caught with the letter. Who shot the fellow?"

"I do not care to say. I do not think it would serve any useful purpose. The fact is—your interests have been protected by murder. Because of that, my friend, I demand a double fee for putting that letter safely in your pocket. Otherwise you and I—and others maybe—might have been turned off by the hangman, as nicely as you please."

"Well, that's as may be. But the matter is serious. Is the murder—known about?"

"It is. But I do not give a fig for the authorities' chances of finding out much about it."

"It is still serious. Do not allow such a thing to happen again."

"Pray do not give me orders. I am no menial—far from it. I am even blessed with some academic accomplishments, or

had you not noticed it? Conduct your own part of the bargain, as I will mine—in whatever way I think fit."

Manners rose slowly to his feet. A sardonic smile spread
evil across his face. "If you are in my pay, sir, you will not
go entirely your own way. Do not forget that a word in the
right place about your—er, activities would bring the authorities about your ears in no time."

"Are you threatening me?" For a moment Adams was incredulous. Then his jaw jutted menacingly. "Do you not forget also that a whisper in the right ear about your very presence in this country could place you before a firing squad
without the grace of a trial."

"Do not be naïve, my friend. Where would you tell them
to find me? 'London,' would you say? London is a big
place."

"Quite, sir. Nor do you know where to find *me*."

Manners took up his cane and smoothed a gloved hand
caressingly down its smooth surface. "That, my friend, is where
you are wrong. Quite wrong. I am not in this dangerous game
for fun. They would not have sent me to this country else. I
have had you followed. I know just where to find you. And
what is more, *Mr. Adams*, do not be so smug about your
assumed name, for *I also know your real one*."

"In the name of the blessed Lord, sir, you have not played
fair."

"I am not here to play fair—though 'tis said all's fair in war,
is it not? Talk of the Lord all you wish, but do not preach
to me of Him. I have my own prayers for Him—and for
France."

Adams rose, his chair crashing over. "All right, I am not
going to tell tales. But I want my fee for this letter I have
had brought out of France."

The man from London took paper from his pocket, sat down
again and reached for a pen on the table. "If you want your
money, sir, then the best way of getting it is to carry another
letter to Roscoff, together with this package of English journals,

which are required there. What I write, you see, will include a request for more money to be sent to me."

Adams made no reply. But he sat down again, sulking while manners opened the letter from France. It read :

> *A01 to Q01. Message A36.*
>
> *Your messages Q24 and Q25 received.*
>
> *The great event for which we all pray and hope for cannot be much longer delayed. This means Ch. information required and Co. information vital.*
>
> *Fishermen not welcome here have slipped our net. They are returning with haul of fish. You as good fisherman yourself see they never fish again, if possible before they can land their haul. Names—M. Guy de Rohan, believed living Wimbledon area; M. Le Comte de St. Brieuc, of Knight's Bridge, London; and M. Paul Rohan-Marichal, of Dover.*
>
>

Do your duty.

Signed A01.
>

When Manners had read the letter he lit the end of it and dropped it into the empty fireplace, watching until it had burned. Then he wrote a reply to the message, and handed it to Adams in a sealed, unaddressed envelope, together with the package of journals.

In the inn yard Manners watched Adams climb up on to his chaise, the envelope in his pocket and the package on the seat beside him.

Then Manners inquired as to the time of the next stage to London. Later, sitting in a corner of that vehicle as it bowled north, his eyes were closed and his face calm, so that the other occupants thought him blissfully and innocently asleep.

But he was thinking of the message he had penned, now on its way to France. It requested money, mentioned the package of journals and ended with these words :

> *Message about unwelcome fishermen understood. **None** shall live.*

CHAPTER NINE

THE LITTLE FERRET struggled back to consciousness as
though he were trying to awaken from a nightmare. He lay on
his back on the damp earth, looking up at the night sky, and
the wind from over the sea chilled his body.

At first the situation in which he found himself was utterly
incomprehensible. He raised his head and lowered it again
because the needles of pain in it jabbed intolerably. But after
a time he lifted himself on an elbow and with difficulty focused
his eyes on one of the rotting limbs of the windmill sail. The
sight refreshed his memory.

Struggling to his feet, he stood dazed and swaying before
staggering a few paces to cling to the side of the door. Now
he remembered all that had happened before his assailant
had struck him down from behind.

He looked about him. The downs were empty of all save
wind and the paling night. Groping into the windmill, he
found that deserted too. Having attacked him, the men had
apparently made off, leaving him to recover.

First the detective searched the windmill. On a table lay
a large lantern which did not appear to have been lit for some
time. In one corner were some small casks, all empty. Opening
a cupboard he found on a dusty shelf a miniature hurricane
lamp, and examining this one he found it had been used quite
recently. Beside it was a piece of cloth with tapes attached to
the sides. It had been daubed with some sort of silvery paint
that in the dark glowed with some luminous quality. On one
side of the piece of fabric, and in the middle of it, two small
straps had been stitched cross-wise. Taking the lamp, Adkins

found that its base fitted more or less securely into the straps.

He closed the cupboard, leaving the articles inside, and sat down for a time on a wooden chair at the table. So the light above the so-called apparition that had raced and circled in the dark had been this lantern, kept in place in the straps on the cloth, which in turn had been tied around a very live animal— judging by its yelps and barks a quite ordinary dog.

So there was nothing ghostly, then, about The Phantom Hound.

He had been somewhat prepared for a simple explanation to the legend of the spectre, having been intrigued with the discovery of the little lantern on his earlier visit.

It was now obvious that some unknown characters—no doubt the smugglers—had created the legend to keep folk away from the spot at night-time.

For the time being the ache in his head made further thought impossible, and he went out and walked down the hill. The fresh breezes cooled his face and he felt a little better.

His horse was still tethered in the copse, and he mounted and rode for Folkestone. Arriving at the customs chief's house in the early hours, he put the animal in the stable, unlocked the little room assigned to him and flung himself on the bed.

The light filtering in the morning through the high, barred window awakened him to clearer senses, and he lay for a time turning over in his mind the events of the previous night.

Methodically, he began his thinking from the beginning. . . .

Firstly, orders for him to be frightened, or attacked if necessary, must have been given by someone who knew his intention to visit the area that night. Who did they include? In the order in which he had told them—Barker, Hackett, Parson Honeycombe, even Fordingham.

Only the last named, he told himself, knew his real identity. But Adkins had learned from his experience as a thieftaker that guessing was no part of logic, and he decided for the time being to remember only that each of the four had been equally aware of his intentions.

Secondly, it seemed the orders had been no more than for him to be given a salutary lesson.

Thirdly, he had chanced on the smugglers' secret cave, and the presence of some casks in the windmill suggested that this building, too, was connected in some way with the free traders.

Fourthly, if he could discover all who had made use of the windmill on the night of the murder, then he might build up a list of those he might suspect of having committed it.

Why, yes, there was one lead. It was a small one, but it was something. Suddenly he remembered that the smugglers in the cave had spoken of an individual who had gone to the windmill on that night. What was his name?

Adkins sprang from the bed, pacing the little room. Bart! Bart, that was the name!

Unfortunately, it sounded like a given and not a surname. But it was better than nothing.

*   *   *

Characteristically, the thieftaker, whose physical actions rarely matched the speed of his brain. dressed slowly in his tailed jacket and pale trousers and patted his top-hat into position on his head.

With his ambling, dignified gait, he moved through the yard to the house to inquire for Fordingham, but he had also slept late, and he learned that the customs chief had already left for his office. Very politely, with a bow and a sweep of his hat, he asked if his horse could be saddled and brought into the yard—not being the man to do such a thing if others were there to do it for him.

Then, mounting, he rode to the *Oddfellows' Arms*, where Barker, the innkeeper, was all simpering concern. "Mr. Adkins, sir, where *have* you been? Worried to death, I've been."

"Why so, Barker, I am in excellent health, as you may perceive, though a trifle hungry." Adkins was smiling widely.

"I should be most pleased if you would have some breakfast sent to my room, together with a pitcher of water and a washing bowl."

Alone in his room and eating cold meats and bread, the detective took from his pocket the notebook he had brought and made a number of entries, he having discovered long ago that the memory is fickle and that the most innocent facts could prove useful when he was engaged on a case.

Barker was hovering in the hall when Adkins came down, his cane under his arm and drawing on his gloves. "Mr. Adkins, sir, what happened to you?" asked the innkeeper. "You was out all night."

"Ah, what indeed?" The detective tapped the side of his nose and winked slyly. "*That* would be telling, my dear fellow."

He walked on, spinning round suddenly as he reached the door. "By the way, Barker," he drawled, "ever heard of an individual by the name of Bart?"

"Can't say as I do, not at the time o' speakin', sir," replied Barker, and no shadow passed across his eyes.

When the thieftaker arrived at the customs house the clerk, having had one experience of this dapper little man's polite but ice-cool determination, informed Mr. Fordingham at once of his presence.

"Ah, Mr. Adkins," said the customs chief, when he was shown in, "how did you fare on your expedition last night?"

Strange that he should be so quick with such a query, thought the detective, eyeing him closely for a moment. But Fordingham was all geniality. Surely it could not have been *him*. Yet few things in the world of crime now surprised the experienced and celebrated thieftaker.

"Got myself much too closely in contact, as it so happens, with a heavy instrument of some sort," he replied, "and I have a lump on my head the size of a duck's egg to show for it."

"Lor', my dear sir, I did tell you to take care, did I not?"

"The deuce you did," said Adkins, drily. "You said, if I remember your precise words, 'Take care not to be found under a hedge.'"

"I may have said as much, though I do not remember it. But Mr. Adkins, sir, who do you think is responsible for this dastardly attack on your person? Who knew you were going there?"

"*You* did."

"But of course, sir. Did you not tell me, and in the most specific terms?"

"You do not allow me to complete my remarks, Mr. Fordingham. I was about to say that you knew—*among others.*" The detective did not voice his knowledge that in the past certain customs officials had been known to be in collusion with the free traders. There had been cases of excise men being bribed to wink the eye, of others who were so afraid of certain smuggling gangs (composed of wanted criminals, highwaymen and common thieves) that they did little or nothing to curb their activities.

What was more, to add to the difficulties of the law officers, many of the public were on the side of the free traders, openly calling them "honest thieves," and approving of their exploits. Why, even soldiers sent to help the revenue men had been known to indulge in smuggling themselves.

All this was known to Adkins, and the facts passed through his mind as Fordingham slowly took a snuff-box from his waistcoat pocket, extracted a liberal pinch and took a long sniff.

"I am much relieved to know I was not—er, the only one to be acquainted with your intentions," said the customs man. "What I had meant to say was—who else knew of them?"

"One or two, sir," said Adkins. "One or two. Now I wonder if you can help me."

"I shall try, Mr. Adkins."

"Well, do you know of any character, one likely to be a smuggler, by the name of Bart?"

"Bart who?"

"Ah, that is the point. 'Tis the only part of the man's name I know—so far."

The revenue man closed his snuff-box with a snap. "I know several gentlemen of that name, all of the highest respectability," he said, "*including myself.*"

The thieftaker was on his feet, his hat toppling from his knees and rolling silently on the floor. "*You* are called Bart?"

"My name," was the reply, "is John Bartholomew Fordingham."

CHAPTER TEN

HARRY ADKINS, being human, had revealed himself to be
startled by the customs chief's disclosure. In addition, also
being human, he was angry with himself for having allowed
his official mask to slip, albeit for a moment. When he had
recovered his hat, rocking on its hard brim on the floor, he
settled himself again on his chair and produced his blandest
smile.

"Bartholomew," he mused. "Not an uncommon name, eh?"

"As you say, Mr. Adkins," said Fordingham, spreading
podgy fingers over his expansive belly. "I must be one of several
bearing it—even in these parts. But why so interested in the
name?"

"I have reason to believe that a man so named may be connected with the smugglers."

"Indeed," declared Fordingham, flashing his most innocent
smile, "I have no idea who that may be. Unless, of course, you
are suspecting *me*."

"I do not, as yet, suspect *anyone*. But I should be most
glad to discover who may be aware already that I am from
Bow Street. I take it, sir, that you have kept faith with me?"

"I have told no one save Lieut. Hogan, of the coast watch,
and——"

"And who?"

"And my wife."

"Ah." The exclamation was delivered with a meaningful
intonation.

"My wife, sir, is of the most trustworthy."

"I am sure she is. But if you will forgive my bluntness, Mr.

Fordingham, the ladies do gossip—never meaning any harm, of course."

"I told her explicitly not to reveal it to a soul."

"If I may be so bold again, Mr. Fordingham, that is sometimes the signal for them to tell the secret to another of their sex at the first opportunity, informing *that* person not to tell a soul."

"I am sorry, then, but I thought my wife——"

"Pray do not give the matter another thought, sir. Now I shall be off to make the acquaintance of Lieutenant Hogan."

"Will you take *him* into your confidence?"

"I rather think I will."

"I am glad of it. I think Hogan could be of the greatest assistance to you."

"I am sure he will do all he can, and of course I shall trust him. If I cannot trust those in authority I am quite sunk in deep water."

"Now if there is any further way in which I can help——"

"There is," said Adkins, preparing to leave. "Continue to keep my real identity secret until I tell you otherwise."

*　　*　　*

On the way to Dymchurch, which he had to pass through on the way to Dungeness, the detective fell to thinking of those whose acquaintance he had already made in the village.

Hackett. A man with a sly smile, who looked at the quiff of your hair instead of your eyes when he talked to you. A tavern keeper who at very least connived with smugglers even if he did not take an active part in their exploits. But not, he imagined, one with the wits to lead them.

Parson Honeycombe. Now there was a strange gentleman. It was not often Adkins could not sum up a man at first meeting. Of Parson Honeycombe the man from Bow Street could so far make nothing.

Susannah Honeycombe. Ah, Susannah. Dainty, appealing, desirable Susannah. For any man who was susceptible to pretty

women, she was disturbing even at first glance. And Adkins
was susceptible to pretty women.

Susannah Honeycombe. Quite the most disturbing person he
had encountered since he arrived, he decided.

There were other cases on which he had worked where
he had been thrown in contact with such women. It had
affected him emotionally—and clouded his judgment. In the
name of God, why did Parson Honeycombe have such an
unexpectedly handsome daughter?

Now there was someone else besides Lieutenant Hogan
from whom he could expect help. The riding officer.

Clopping into Dymchurch, he set about inquiring for Mr.
Quested, the apothecary. The gentleman was a well-known
worthy of the town, and his shop was soon pointed out.

An assistant showed him to an upstairs room overlooking
the narrow hight street, and here Adkins found his man poring
over his accounts. It was quite a large room and well appointed.
The desk at which the apothecary sat was of beech grained
to look like fashionable rosewood. Above the polished steel
grate was a marble mantelpiece, evidence that this office had
once been a living room over the shop.

"Mr. Adkins of London," announced the shop assistant,
closing the door and leaving.

Quested at once politely bundled his ledgers and papers into
the drawer of the desk and rose to extend a large hand. The
thieftaker's size made the apothecary seem to tower over him,
but the smile he received was wide and welcoming.

"Mr. Adkins, of Bow Street," he said to the visitor. "How
do you do, sir?"

"How d'you do?" replied the detective.

"Pray take a seat, Mr. Adkins. You will be fatigued after
your journey from London."

"Oh, I did not come from London today, Mr. Quested,"
smiled Adkins. "I have been here some few days and have
quite recovered from the journey."

The Runner sat down on an elegant black and gold sofa.

"If I may say so, sir," he began, "you are astonishing quick at assuming that I am from Bow Street. I do not think I had as yet informed you of my profession."

" 'Tis easy, Mr. Adkins. The only person I was expecting from London was a man from Bow Street. It was I, you see, who asked that you be sent for."

"Indeed, sir."

"I take it you have already made the acquaintance of Mr. Customer Fordingham?"

"I have."

"Then did he not tell you it was my suggestion you should be sent for?"

"I cannot say I recall his making such a statement, Mr. Quested."

"The sly old devil." The apothecary appeared much amused, and Adkins thought his smile of the frankest. "Taking all the credit to himself, eh? Well, it does not matter. The main thing is to get results from your visit, and the sooner the better the way things are going."

"I am glad to see, then, Mr. Quested, that there are others here besides our Mr. Fordingham who are concerned about law and order."

" 'Tis not unnatural. My business is to do with law and order—or did Mr. Fordingham not tell you that either. I am not only a shopkeeper, sir. I am also a riding officer."

The man's broad smile was infectious, and Adkins's own face was soon creasing in sympathy with the fellow.

"Fordingham did tell me that much," grinned the thief-taker.

"I've been a riding officer this many a year, and if I may be so bold, Mr. Adkins, I'm one of the most conscientious in these parts. I have the time for it, you see, on account of my having no less than two assistants to look to my business here. In a manner of speaking, sir, it is somewhat of a hobby of mine—not letting the free traders have it all their own way."

"Excellent. Now what can you tell me about the murder?"

"So far—not much I am afraid. I have been asking some questions around, pending your arrival, but there is some suggestion that the poor midshipman was murdered on a night when a run was taking place—and I might say the smugglers have the people around here greatly terrified. It is difficult to loosen tongues."

"You have not told any that a thieftaker was coming from London?"

"I have not. I knew nothing of your methods. I am sufficient of a riding officer to know that a man must make his inquiries in his own way."

"You are a splendid fellow," said the visitor, his eyes gleaming, "and I think we shall get on splendidly."

"I do my best. 'Tis not easy. Such riding officers as there are have their own businesses to attend to as well as patrolling the coast, and what are a mere handful against the hundreds who are involved when it comes to a run—and many more hundreds who connive at their devilry?"

"There is but one answer, Mr. Quested. We must have better wits than they—and keep our brains a-dancing. At the moment I am on my way to talk with Lieutenant Hogan, of the coast watch, and I would wish to return this way before dark. But I shall come to see you again, now that I have made your acquaintance. We shall join forces on this task."

"You may rest assured I shall do my best for you. I, at least, am not afraid of the smugglers."

They shook hands on the bargain, and Adkins went out through the shop.

Riding further down the coast towards Dungeness, Adkins felt more relaxed than at any time since his arrival. Meeting Quested had been in the nature of a tonic, for the man spoke as one who cared a great deal for law and order and would go to great lengths to preserve it. He would appear to do more even than the customs chief.

Why, he was not so sure now of Fordingham, and since his last meeting with him he had been feeling more lonely than at

any time since his arrival. But now he had met Quested. And
Ransome Quested was forthright and free of speech and had a
winning way with him.

*   *   *

When the thieftaker came to the watch house he was challenged by a naval rating armed with a carbine, but was shown
in to Lieutenant Hogan as soon as he gave his name.

"I was expecting you, Mr. Adkins," said the lieutenant.
" 'Fraid this post is no palace, but pray take the most comfortable seat we have to offer."

The visitor lowered himself into an old wooden armchair
innocent of cushioning, and the officer took his hat, gloves and
cane.

"At least you have an excellent view of the sea," observed
Adkins, taking shrewd stock of the officer and noting he was
tall and lithe with an intelligent face, and that he smiled with
his eyes as well as his mouth.

"That," said Hogan, his eyes still twinkling, "is why they
built the place here. My job is to keep watch over the sea for
many things, and these days for what we do not want to see—
French men-o'-war. But I do not fancy that is what you came
to talk about. It will be about poor Harrington?"

"Correct, lieutenant. I am here to find his murderer."

"And with all my heart, sir, I wish you every success. Allow
me to say at once that I shall furnish you with all the help at
my disposal. If you wish to interview the ratings who accompanied Harrington on that night, just say the word."

"Yes, I should like to see them."

"I shall attend to that, and if you require armed men, they
shall be at your command."

Adkins smiled wryly. "My thanks to you. I may need a
show of strength eventually. Not, however, for the time being.

"For one thing, I do not take kindly to the sight of firearms.
They are regrettably most necessary in our world today, but
I think them most dangerous articles to have about the place.

"For another, I find that the sight of them can seal lips as tight as oyster shells."

"Very well. But before you are done, Mr. Adkins, you may need my men for your own protection."

"I do not doubt it, lieutenant. Already I have been banged about the head and left for senseless not ten miles from this very spot. If I can discover who found such a course necessary—well, sir, I shall be a step nearer my goal. In the meantime, have you any theory that may fit the murder of Mr. Harrington?"

"As to that, my thoughts must be similar to your own. It is certain that there was a run taking place that night, and the blockaders interfered with their little games. I should say it was a free trader who fired the shot. But there are so many o' them in these parts that one cannot guess who is one o' them and who is not."

"That I am beginning to discover. Now can you tell me if you have had any visitors in the past few weeks who may have spoken of violence—or the need for it?"

"I cannot say that I have. Violence? Not that I can remember. But wait, sir, for if by violence one could mean war, then I have, sir."

"I was not meaning war, but pray continue——"

"I have had a gentleman here offering help to throw the French back into the sea. That gentleman was Parson Honeycombe, of Dymchurch. The cleric, it would appear, knows every free trader by name, and he offered to lead the cutthroats himself if the French do land. But that is not the violence of *murder*."

"It is not. But it's a deuced strange offer for a parson to make. Lieutenant, what you tell me is fascinating. Incredible almost. I shall make a note of it, for it may turn out to fit the puzzle."

"Well, the offer has put me to much thinking, I must say. D'you know, the reverend gentleman looks as though he could give a good account of himself with a weapon."

"For your information, my friend, I have already had the pleasure of meeting your Parson Honeycombe, and damme if I can make the fellow out."

"Nor more can I, Mr. Adkins, though I have accepted his offer."

"Well, if the French do come, I suppose he'd be more use with a pistol in his hand than preaching fire from the pulpit." The detective rose and looked out over the sea. "I met the cleric's daughter also," he mused. "An unlikely daughter for such a raw-boned giant."

"Do not be so sure about that," said Lieutenant Hogan, grinning broadly. "I have spoken with her—aye, and danced with her—at the best assemblies in Folkestone. Looks as though butter wouldn't melt in her mouth—I'll give you that—but they say she's a wild 'un all right. Got the spirit of her father, if the tales be true."

From the face of Harry Adkins the smile had gone. "In—what way, sir?"

The officer's eye closed in a slow wink. "They say she knows all about it," he said, somewhat inconclusively.

"All about—what?"

"Well, you know. Can't speak from first hand, Mr. Adkins, for she hasn't favoured me. But they say she's free o' her charms, though none dare say it if Honeycombe's around to hear it. She's said to mix with known smugglers—though that would not be difficult as her pa's choir is full o' them—and there's not one wouldn't give a crock o' gold to bed her."

"Do you realize what you are saying—her the daughter of a parson?"

"Parson's daughter or not, she's made the same as any wench. If the tales be true, she's been seduced more times than she's had good dinners—and I warrant they eat well at the vicarage.

"They do say that Ransome Quested, the riding officer, is paying court to her like a lovesick boy who's just awakened to the fascinating difference between male and female——"

" 'Tis their affair." Adkins, who heaven knew was no prude, stood rigidly to attention, his hat and cane snatched from the table. "I thank you most cordially for your help, and I shall be back to see you again."

"A moment, sir. You wanted me to send for the ratings?"

"I have changed my mind." The thieftaker was speaking slowly and with some deliberation. "I do not feel much in the mood for interviewing at the moment. I shall see them some other time."

"As you wish. I am at your service."

They clasped hands firmly, having taken a distinct liking to each other, and it was to be regretted, perhaps, that the lieutenant had volunteered quite so much information.

"I do say, Mr. Adkins, that I shall look forward to helping you to run down the murderer."

"Thank you. I shall have need of you." The detective, despite the strange shock he had sustained, returned Hogan's frank smile.

"And as for the—er, gallivanting of the vicar's daughter," added the thieftaker, "I do not think that will have much bearing on my inquiries. I do not think I am greatly interested in Miss Susannah Honeycombe."

Returning to Dymchurch, plodding his unhurried way, his thoughts, for once not entirely on his work, belied that final statement he had made about the lady. There was something he was not yet fully aware of, and he was grateful for the solitary downs and the lonely road, for they allowed his mind some freedom of reflection.

CHAPTER ELEVEN

THE LANDLORD OF the *Oddfellows' Arms* waited for Adkins's return agog with news, and the moment his guest arrived he drew him mysteriously into an empty parlour.

"So you want excitement, eh?" he said. "You want a diversion? You and your talk o' nuthin' ever 'appening in these parts. Well, there's bin a murder, sir—a foul murder in Dover. Now wot d'yer think o' that, sir?"

"Indeed, Barker. Well, that's a turn-up, eh? Am I interested? Of course I am. Dover, eh? But a stride down the road, if I'm not much mistaken."

"No more'n six mile up the coast, sir."

"Well, speak up, man. Who is it? Who's been done in this time?"

"Don't know 'is name, Mr. Adkins. Can't rightly remember it. Furrin-soundin' name it were, see? But a gentleman by all accounts."

"D'you know anything of the circumstances?"

"Circumstances?"

"How it happened?"

It was obvious by the animation on Barker's face that he was going to relish recounting the details of the case. "'Appened this very mornin', it did. While it were still dark. 'Twould seem he'd answered a knocking on his door, for they found 'im dead as mutton on 'is own doorstep in a great pool of blood, with a 'orrible wound in the chest. They say he must 'ave bin shot at point-blank range."

"Point-blank, eh?"

"Aye."

"H'm." Adkins replaced his hat thoughtfully, and began to draw on his gloves again. "Getting to be a habit round here, folk getting shot in the chest from very close range."

"How d'yer mean?"

"Well, that's *precisely* what happened to Mr. Midshipman Harrington, was it not? I should like you to lend me a fresh horse, Barker. I've a mind to trot over there, for a diversion you understand."

Barker scurried about instructing an ostler to saddle a horse for "the gentleman", and entreating his guest to take care as it would no doubt be dark before his return. The landlord was pleased to be providing "an excitement" for his guest, and even hoping—for he was a businessman almost to the exclusion of all else—that the murder might in some strange and macabre way bring notoriety to this coast and morbid sightseers seeking bed and breakfast.

Arriving at Dover in the twilight, Adkins went at once to the chief citizen of the town and made his name and office known to him.

"Your presence is most fortuitous, Mr. Adkins, though I am at a loss to understand why you are here, for no request has been made to Bow Street," said that personage, whose name was Gillingham.

"I am not here officially, so do not raise your hopes too high," explained the Runner. "I am in fact investigating a case of murder some twenty miles away, and I came to see you because there would appear to be a similarity in the two crimes."

The murder had taken place much as Barker had described it. The victim's manservant had been away for the night visiting relatives, and the gentleman of the house had answered the early-morning knocking himself. Neighbours had been awakened by a noise, but had not ventured out until early light, and the assailant, whoever he was, had got clean away.

Now the murdered man was a Frenchman named *Paul Rohan-Marichal*. He had been an *émigré* to England at the time of the French Revolution and a member of one of those staunchly royalist families of Brittany who had held out for long against the rampaging *sans-culottes*, then come to England to do whatever could still be done against the new regime.

These Frenchmen who still worked against their country's new order had gained for themselves the proud name of *Les Chouans*. They had formed, Adkins knew, the last pocket of French resistance to the revolution. Of Celtic origin, speaking their own native patois not unlike the Welsh tongue, they were a long, stinging stiletto in Napoleon's side, and one he could not ignore. Adkins was aware that they were now sometimes used by the British intelligence services in the war with France.

"This man," asked Adkins, "do you know anything of his movements of late?"

"He had just returned from a journey when this happened. Said he'd been to visit friends. His manservant says he was about to make a further journey, this time to London."

"Did he still have any connections—with France?"

"If he had, he never spoke of them."

"No," breathed Adkins, "I should not have expected him to. Mr. Gillingham, when was the first coach out of Dover after this happened, and where did it go?"

"It left from *The Dover Stage* about an hour after the murder. It was the London coach."

"Mr. Gillingham, I shall ask a question or two at *The Dover Stage*. Then I shall post to London, and I think you may find that when I return I shall know a little more about M'sieur Paul Rohan-Marichal. You may find I may be working on this case also."

Unhurried and unflurried, as was his way, Adkins took a turn down the road to *The Dover Stage*, where he set about making laconic inquiries. He learned that only four passengers had taken seats in the morning coach. Three of them were ladies, travelling together and booked to Canterbury. The fourth was a gentleman no one could recall ever having seen.

He, too, had paid a single fare to Canterbury, but had not seemed to be connected in any way with the three ladies. In fact, he had appeared as from nowhere in the inn yard a few minutes before the guard put his post-horn to his lips, and had scarcely time to arrange his journey.

"I should like a full description of the fellow," said Adkins. "Tall or short? Complexion? Dress? Anything you can remember. The merest detail even."

The thieftaker spoke to everyone who remembered having seen the man. Then, retiring to a quiet corner of the inn parlour, he wrote this in his notebook:

Early morning coach. Complete stranger. Tall, some say over six feet. Pale face. Clean-shaven. Some say dark eyes, others think thick, black eyebrows. Not seen to smile or pass time of day, but dress and manner of a gentleman. Dress: long, dark coat of type used for riding, black top-hat, cane. Speech: brusque, precise.

He closed the note-book, opened it again, shrugged his shoulders and added: *This as far as I can judge. Why can't people remember the same thing the same way?*

Next he inquired as to the time of the London coach early the following day, and mounted his borrowed horse to return to Folkestone for the night.

He went in no great haste, for the most part allowing the animal to pick its own way on the lonely, darkening road. The wind was rising, setting the clouds to sailing, bending the willows near the marshland and ruffling his thoughts.

Harry Adkins thought best when he was warm and comfortable and contented, and at the moment he was none of these. It seemed a queer, puckish quirk of life that a man such as he should have chosen a profession where often he had to stand for hours on windy street corners, travel great distances in discomfort and come in contact with criminals and their weapons, and he possessed a secret horror for both. But the time would come, in the days of greying hair, when he would realize that it was the troubles and worries and not the joys and happinesses that life was all about.

He was a long way, he knew, from discovering the man who had murdered the midshipman, and a longer way still from taking him. Now there was a complication, another killing committed in much the same way.

This latter crime may have no bearing on his particular assignment. But to be thorough it must be followed up.

At the *Oddfellows' Arms* he told the landlord that he would be making a journey very early in the morning and would not be returning to the inn the following night.

"But I shall be back," he said. "Reserve a room for me against my return and keep charge of my valise."

At Dover the next day he joined the same London coach that the strange, dark-clothed gentleman had taken, and like him booked a seat to Canterbury. Arriving there, he made inquiries about a tall, unsmiling gentleman who had arrived "by this coach yesterday and at this very hour".

Yes, sir, they remembered him. Arrived with three ladies, he had. *They* had ended their journey there, but *he* had booked on to London, loitering in the yard until the horses were changed.

"Then I should like to travel on to London in this coach," said Adkins.

"Not possible, sir," said the guard. "Booked up, sir. Booked right up. Passengers joining the coach here."

"I am afraid I shall have to get to London—and rather quickly," explained the thieftaker.

"Can't be did, sir. Sorry, sir."

"I would ask you to find a way of getting me on to this coach. There's a good fellow." Adkins took a coin from his pocket, spun it in the air and caught it.

"Not for an 'undred pounds, sir."

"I do not wish to argue, my good man. But I must inform you that I am a peace officer from Bow Street and I travel on the authority of the chief magistrate."

"Can't 'elp 'oo you travel fer."

"Do not beat about the bush, man. I travel on this coach. Inside, outside, beside the driver or in the boot. Please yourself where."

"Don't know as 'ow———"

"What is your name?"

"Find out."

"What is your name?"

"Wot d'yer want ter know fer?"

"So that, *if I do not travel in your coach*, I shall see to it that you answer to Sir Richard Ford, of Bow Street, the Secretary for War and the First Lord of the Admiralty. In any case, I shall find your name quite easily, but you try my patience not telling me at once."

"Me name's 'Epplethwaite."

"Thank you. Now Mr. Hepplethwaite, on which part of your coach do I travel?"

"Squeeze yer in up top, then."

"What a splendid fellow you are, Mr. Hepplethwaite. I had thought of putting this coin back into my pocket. Put it in yours instead—and find me two rugs. *Two* rugs. I've travelled atop before."

*   *   *

Alighting from the coach in London, Adkins made at once for Bow Street, where he reported to Sir Richard Ford the murder of Monsieur Paul Rohan-Marichal.

The magistrate listened grave-faced, waiting for Adkins to finish his account. "It is well that you have returned to tell me of this," he said then, "for I have two items of intelligence that match your own identically. Your M'sieur Rohan-Marichal is not the only Frenchman to have met with sudden death."

"There are others?"

"Two. Before I breakfasted the day before yesterday I was informed that M'sieur Guy de Rohan was shot in the back as he arrived at his home in Wimbledon from a journey. He had rung the door bell and was waiting for it to be opened for him. As his servant was drawing the bolts within he heard the explosion of a pistol, and as he flung open the door he heard the sound of running feet in the early morning. De Rohan's assailant was fast disappearing with his back to the servant, who had no chance of seeing what manner of man he was. He did not give chase, for his first thought was to assist his master, but nothing further could be done for the poor fellow."

"And the other, Sir Richard?"

"M'sieur Le Comte de St. Brieuc. The same day. He had ordered a phaeton to call at his lodgings in Knight's Bridge to visit the building of the Secretary for War. Passers-by gave accounts of how a coach with its blinds drawn halted further down the street, pointing in the same direction as that in which St. Brieuc would move off. St. Brieuc left the house, walked down the steps and began to climb into the open carriage. At the same time the coach began to move and as it drew level a hand clutching a pistol appeared from the curtained window. Whoever occupied the coach must have had at least two loaded pistols,, for there were two shots, both most accurate, and the victim received a ball in the chest and another in the head. He died instantly."

"And the coach?"

"It was found abandoned in the Old Brompton Road. It had been stolen. Its discovery brought us no clue."

"Is the whole thing a complete mystery, then?"

"Not entirely. We know *why* they were killed. Both had been on a journey to France. They had gone—and not for the first time—to assist our intelligence service. They had hoped to contact friends in Brittany and learn matters about the French war that would have been of considerable interest to England. And now it will never be known what facts they brought back locked up inside their heads. Both were killed before they could report to they who knew of their errand."

"Then I suspect the same applies to the poor fellow at

Dover," declared Adkins. "He was about to make a journey to London."

Sir Richard rose from his chair, drumming his fingers on his desk. "I should think you are perfectly correct," he said. "These three murders are no doubt the work of a French agent who skulks here in England under our very noses. Who is he? How do we track him down?"

"And more important, Sir Richard, how did he know so quickly that these brave members of *Les Chouans* had been across the water and come back again?"

"*That* is the question. A damned urgent one, too. They are no ordinary murders these. A midshipman gets killed interfering with smugglers on the coast. That's one thing. But the deaths of these three men sent secretly into France? That is quite another. My dear Adkins, I am off this instant to the Office of War. Wait here against my return. You may find that within the hour you are retained by the government as well as the customs service."

CHAPTER TWELVE

To PASS THE time until Sir Richard returned, Harry Adkins strolled across the street to the *Brown Bear*, which lay opposite the Bow Street Public Office, to take a drink with John Clark, one of his fellow thieftakers.

"Anything of note occurred while I've been away?" he asked his colleague, ordering two glasses of geneva. "Bring me up to date with the gossip, there's a good fellow."

"You've returned just at the right moment to be acquainted with an item of news, and by Jehoshaphat it's as startling as anything you'll hear in a twelvemonth. We thieftakers of Bow Street now number five instead of six."

"Lor' save us!" exclaimed Adkins. "The six of us were few enough for all the work there is to do. London's a cesspool of crime. What's happened, eh?"

"Jeremy's gone. Been sent packing by the magistrates. Relieved of his office of thieftaker."

"In the name of God, John, why?"

"Drink your gin and I'll tell you," said Clark, producing a couple of pennies for two more drinks. "You know the rules." Clark began to quote: *"The thieftakers are all men of tried courage, picked from among the peace officers, and the moment any of them commits an act of cruelty or injustice he is immediately discharged and never admitted again.* Remember the clause?"

"Of course, John. I know it like my own name."

"Well, Jeremy's fallen foul of it."

"It's the clause in our employment that makes us angry whenever the public, as they do so often, call us foul names because they don't like the idea of Sir Richard's police patrols and his prying Runners. But what has Jeremy done?"

"He lost his temper while interviewing a suspect and used blows to make him confess. The man Jeremy cornered is as rotten a core of humanity as ever trod the cesspit of Whitefriars. But Jeremy's conduct towards him has been proved, and Sir Richard has let the criminal go scot-free—and sent our colleague packing."

"Poor Jeremy. You and I, John, can understand there are times when we feign would lose our tempers. We can understand it well. But Jeremy knew the rules. He has no redress."

"No, he has not. 'Tis a lesson for all of us. One of the foot patrol will be promoted to thieftaker to take his place, and that will be that. Now what other news have I? Ah, yes, I have had a success, Harry, while you have been taking the sea air——"

"Taking the sea air indeed! Pshaw! Getting knocked on the head while doing so. Damn sight safer in London. Well, what have you been complimented on, Harry?"

"I conducted a most successful raid on a molly-house."

"Ah, yes, one of those strange establishments where homosexual folk meet?"

"The same. Caught a dozen of them in the act, and I'm afraid some o' my men kicked 'em about a bit on the rump. But never a word about that or I'll be going the same way as poor Jeremy."

"Not a whisper," smiled Adkins. "Have these homos been tried yet?"

"Aye—and all found guilty."

"Congratulations, John. Then they will have been sentenced to death?"

"Aye, they'll be hanged by the neck until they're as dead as roasted geese, for that's the sentence for homosexuality. But I'm afraid it's me doing all the boasting. What of you, Harry? How do you progress at the seaside? Taken your murderer yet?"

"Taken him?" Adkins smiled ruefully. "I've as much notion who he is as how many wenches have been bedded out of wedlock."

"You'll get him."

"I'd like to think so."

"You always do."

"Flatterer. S'pose you want me to buy you another gin? Well, we'll make it a quick 'un. Sir Richard might be driving back to the office this very minute."

"All right, get your pennies on the table and I'll hail the landlord."

Soon the two were back in the police office, tilting back in their chairs and resting their feet on a table as they awaited the return of the magistrate, and Adkins, warmed by the geneva he had drunk, told a little of his progress—or lack of it—on the south coast : "All I can say is that I must find a man named Bart, who I think may know more of the affair than he would care to speak of, that he may well be the killer, that the murder is connected in some way with the free traders, that it is any-body's guess who is implicated in smuggling and who is not, and that the smugglers have it all their own way, either be-cause they are feared or because folk think the customs duties are an imposition and that to evade them is fair sport.

"I have also come across the most unlikely cleric I have ever met, a man who vows to fight the Frenchies with his own hands if they should land and knows all the smugglers by their Christian names.

"Now the parson has a daughter in whose pretty mouth you wouldn't think butter would melt, but who is, if folk be right, one o' the most harem-scarum young wenches in many a long mile."

"Oh ho ! Pretty is she ?"

"Don't know if pretty's the right word, but there's some-thing about her face—aye and all the other interesting parts of her—that fair haunts me. Put her in satin and diamonds, sit her in a duke's drawing-room for a soirée and every swaggering blood in town would give his sword arm to carry her off to bed."

Clark grinned waggishly. "Harry, you old seducer. You desire her. Come on, you old rake, admit it."

"Maybe so," said Adkins, avoiding his friend's eyes. "But maybe more than that—this time."

"Well, we earn enough to keep a lady in some style, should we wish to wed. Our pay here, our fees and expenses when the public engage us, it all adds up to a respectable sum in a year. Then there's our share of the £40 distributed among the witnesses when we procure a conviction. Reckon we make anything up to £40 a year from that alone. What's stopping you from asking the lady to marry you?"

"For one thing, I've spoken no more than a dozen polite words to her. But for another, damme, I'm too uneasy about her strange father. God grant that he is not implicated in the murder. But it is not a good thing for me to be thinking so, Harry. We should preserve an open mind on such things. Damn the woman!"

"What? You'd curse a pretty wench?"

"Aye, damn her. I cannot think straight because of her."

* * *

Sir Richard Ford returned to Bow Street with an air of briskness and gravity, and at once called both Adkins and Clark into his office.

"We are to put our minds to a matter of great importance," he began. "I speak of the murders of the three French *émigrés*. These crimes are viewed with the greatest alarm. An official of the Office of War is at this moment with the editor of *The Times*, imploring him to be careful what he publishes about the murders. An account of each is to be printed so as to allay suspicion on the part of the murderer, but they will appear as separate items and will not be connected in any way. Other journals will be asked to co-operate in the same way."

"A good move," said Adkins.

"In the meantime, we are to find as quickly as possible the French snake that lurks in our English grasses, for our military intelligence service believes that one such must exist and that it must be he who is the killer.

"He must be found—and quickly.

"This task I assign to you two gentlemen, and your services are to be retained by the government.

"Now I warn you that it will not be like searching for an ordinary thieving murderer who scurries away to his pit in Whitefriars. This man of whom I speak will be one of the cleverest spies the armies of France can produce. He will also be dangerous—to us who are to seek him and to the security of the country."

"We shall do our best," said Adkins.

"I know you will. You, Mr. Adkins, are already involved, for you have come in with news of the death of the *émigré* at Dover. I should like you to return to the south coast and continue your investigations into the murder of the midshipman, and at the same time look into the death of M'sieur Rohan-Marichal. It is not impossible, as you suggest yourself, that they are in some way connected."

"I will go at once," said Adkins.

"You, Mr. Clark, I should like you to inquire into the two murders that have taken place in London. Consult each other if necessary, by letter or visit, and spare no expense or effort. You must both feel free to conduct your inquiries in whatever way you think fit, and I shall not worry you with the necessity of reporting back to me if it should in any way interfere with your work.

"Good luck, gentlemen. I need not tell you—with the French threatening to reach out at our throats across the Channel— how vital your task will be."

CHAPTER THIRTEEN

THE LITTLE FERRET burrowed back to the Kent coast and its web of intrigue. He drove into Folkestone in a fast curricle, as a gentleman of influence would drive in his own carriage, the difference being that the vehicle was on hire for as long as it may be required, and the man at the reins was a captain of foot patrol at Bow Street, dressed inconspicuously to resemble a manservant and assigned to remain under the detective's orders for as long as he may be needed.

This time there lay locked in the boot of the curricle a carbine, a cutlass and a pair of pistols. These were the normal equipment of the man acting the part of driver, and he knew how to use them, if the thieftaker did not. This time Harry Adkins, sitting top-hatted and nonchalant, was not quite so light-hearted as his supercilious air might have suggested.

His companion, one Richard Elias, a man normally in charge of a street patrol of four, felt a little out of his accustomed sphere, but as an officer of phlegmatic and loyal disposition, and a member of a force which had a high regard for its celebrated thieftaker, he was prepared to take any events connected with the adventure as they came.

They came to Folkestone in the fading light, with a grey mist rising on the windless sea and a half-brother of a haze creeping among the mastheads. Later, when the day died and the lamps were lit, the slow, curling fingers of sea-vapour would invade the town, obscuring the ships' riding lights as they stole by. The fog would come insidiously, so that no one would seem to realize it was there until the light from an unshuttered window would no longer shine but merely glow.

The silence would become strange and the sound of a footfall or a cough uncanny. And already there was a stillness.

It pervaded the yard of the *Oddfellows' Arms* as the curricle drew in and halted. This strange silence, and their knowledge of mysterious events, made its two occupants shiver a little as if winter came too early. Adkins descended and ambled across the cobbles into the inn, looking for Barker the landlord.

"Ah, Mr. Adkins, sir, so you are back again," said Barker, making an unnecessary point.

"As you can see, Barker, as you can see," replied the thief-taker, his air of superior calm hiding a new excitement. "This time I have brought my own curricle—and my own man. Thought I'd appreciate the countryside the better. Trust you can accommodate both of them?"

"For you, Mr. Adkins, of course I can."

"Thank you, Barker. Now what have you got to tempt me? Roast beef a trifle rare? Game pie? A capon's leg or wing, eh? I should like the best you've got, and my man will eat with me also. He has driven many a mile."

Lounging in the parlour's most comfortable chair after his meal and sipping smuggled brandy, for his expenses allowed him to live well on an assignment, Adkins did not that night do any active work, though his mind was not at rest for a moment.

The next day he decided to visit Lieutenant Hogan and ask if he may interview the four ratings who had accompanied the midshipman on the night of the run.

From them he learned that their ill-fated officer had walked to the windmill alone, sending them to the cliff-top because a solitary figure had left the beach and made his way towards the windmill. This man, no doubt, would be "Bart."

"Describe the fellow, if you please?"

"Don't know as I can," replied one of the ratings. "It was dark and a long way off. He were just—a man."

"Did you hear a shot from the direction of the wind-mill?"

"Couldn't have done, sir. There was a lot o' shootin' a-goin' on at cliff-top."

"Can you remember anything about the man at all? Was he tall, short, did he limp, strut, stride?"

"I'd say he were not all that tall. But a heavy man, I'd say. Yes, heavy. He just walked quickly to the windmill, without stopping for a moment, as though he were in the habit of going there, if you gets my meaning, sir."

"I do. Well, thank you, and if you recall anything further about that night—anything at all, remember—then tell it to Lieutenant Hogan here. And now, lieutenant, I must be off. Any message you may wish to send would get me at the *Odd-fellows' Arms* at Folkestone."

"Right. Now please remember, Mr. Adkins, any assistance you should require, armed or otherwise, do not hesitate to let me know."

The thieftaker left with this comforting assurance from Lieutenant Hogan, and ordered Elias to drive the curricle to Dymchurch.

Arrived there, Adkins left Elias outside *The Ship*, himself entering to find landlord Hackett.

"I didn't have a pleasant visit to the windmill," remarked Adkins.

"Warned yer, didn't I?"

"Must say you did."

"Ugh!" Hackett simulated awe and fear. "Devil 'as the place fer 'is own, reckon. A proper witches' den it is."

"It was no witch knocked me over the head."

"Got banged about the 'ead, eh?" This time Hackett feigned surprise.

"Had a lump as big as a duck's egg to show for it."

"You don't say?"

"I do say. Know anything about it?"

"W'y ask me, Mr. Adkins, sir?"

"It may interest you to know that you were one of only *three persons* who knew I was to make the visit."

"Well, ask the other two. I ain't done nuthin'. Bet yer all the rum in the King's Navy it were a witch——"

"Witch be damned! Do not trifle with me, man, and do not take me for a fool. I might add that I have some considerable influence, both here and in London Town. I advise you to be careful what you say, and think carefully before you answer my next question—do you know of any man who goes by the name of Bart?"

Hackett drew an involuntary breath. "Bart?"

"You heard the name quite correctly."

Hackett lowered himself into a chair, thinking hard. "Got me there you 'ave. If there's a man called Bart 'e don't drink 'is ale 'ere. Do you think it were a man named Bart wot 'it you?"

"I did not say that."

Hackett rose to his feet again. He had recovered from his shock, and his face was dark and scowling. "Leave us alone, can't yer mister. I don't know why you're so bloody interested, but we don't like toffs from Lunnon proddin' about an' pokin' their noses around. 'Twas good advice I gave yer about goin' ter the windmill at midnight, wern't it? Take my advice again. Flog off back to Lunnon where yer came from."

"Pray do not have an apopletic, my good fellow," drawled Adkins, twirling his ebony cane in gloved fingers. "I shall take my leave of you before you are quite put off your own ale. But before I go, I should like to say that I am damned interested in your excitement. What have you got to hide, Hackett? I should also like to say this—do not dare to tell me what to do, for I shall do precisely as I please and stay here a twelve-month if I should so fancy." At the door he paused, turned and added in casual and sarcastic tones: "Don't forget that tub of cheap brandy will you, Hackett, or I shall take it much amiss."

Next he visited another tavern, *The City of London*. In the taproom he raised a tankard to his lips, surveyed a half-dozen farm workers dressed in smocks and announced in a loud firm voice: "Can any of you good people help me? I am looking for a man by the name of Bart. Can any of you help me to find him?"

Conversation in the room ceased as though he had sounded the knell of doom. Tankards, drained quickly, were banged down. All eyes were upon him. Not a word was spoken. One by one, the tavern's customers slunk out into the street.

At last the thieftaker and the landlord eyed each other alone.

"Strange," commented Adkins.

"Aye," said the landlord.

"Strangest behaviour I ever did see," continued the police officer.

" 'Appen it is," said the landlord.

"Have a drink with me," offered the detective.

"No," said the landlord, "thankee."

Back in the curricle, Adkins took off his top-hat, planted it more firmly on his head and said: "Right, Captain Elias, we shall now pay a call on the vicar."

Passing under the little arched gateway, where the latch had long ceased to work, Adkins paused to study Parson Honeycombe's house.

The years had darkened its timbers and the seasons laid patterns of moss on its roof. The path was but trodden earth, winding where the feet of centuries had skirted tree and bush. This led downwards, through the uncut grasses, for the vicarage lay in a hollow, in the shadow of the church and the old, old trees. In some strange way, it seemed to nestle in its own shadow. When the mists came its top would float in winter's foam.

The house was at least Elizabethan, probably earlier. It was a place that seemed to have gone to sleep a long time ago. It was of an age that had secrets that never were told.

The look of the place gave the detective a feeling of uneasiness, and he walked back to the curricle. "A precaution,

Captain Elias," he said. "Do not leave the buggy outside the gate. Hide it—and yourself—up the road there in the shade of that clump of trees."

Parson Honeycombe received Adkins most politely, asking if he would care to take a dish of tea. "You are apparently taking an extended holiday in these parts?" he suggested.

"I have not, as it happens, seen the Kent coast before," replied Adkins. "I am afraid I have shut myself away too long in London and did not previously know of the delights of your coast resorts."

"How long do you plan to remain here, Mr. Adkins?"

"For a spell, vicar, for a spell."

"I hope you are enjoying your stay, sir?"

"It is most agreeable, vicar. But I must say—you have some quaint folk in this little parish of yours."

"Oh, what engenders such a remark, sir, if I may be so bold?"

"Well, I was told there was a man here named Bart, who is quite a character by all accounts and who could tell me some fascinating stories. I keep an album of such. 'Tis a hobby of mine. But whenever I mention the fellow's name, folk look at me as I have the plague and go their ways without a murmur. Not one will tell me where to find him."

"Well, sir, *I* shall make no mystery of it. I should say you refer to a man by the name of Barley, baptized Bartholomew, a member of my flock, you know. Vicar's warden, in fact, but on occasion he's missed a Sunday or two, on account of he does a spot of seafaring. Not that he does much of that, though, for he gets violently sick at sea and more than once I have advised him against sailing with a vessel. If you would like to see him I shall have him brought to the vicarage and we can chat to him together."

"Pray do not go to such trouble, vicar, for if you will but tell me where to find him——"

" 'Tis no trouble, and 'twould be better my way. He is indeed a character. Odd man, really. Don't suppose he would talk to you at all unless I were present, and I think he is some-where around the church at the moment."

"Can you explain the villagers' shyness with regard to the fellow?"

"Only that there are strange stories on this coast. Believe me, sir, half the tales are not true, but the village folk think every man who sets foot on land from a ship has something about his person with which he is trying to evade customs duty. There have been stories about Bartholomew. I do not believe them to be true."

"Stories about folk can be odd, can they not, vicar? For instance, I heard one about you."

"Oh? What, pray?"

"That you know that many of your congregation indulge in free trading, that you are aware they have weapons to hand in their homes, and that you have offered to lead them against French troops that might land on this coast."

"Ah, yes, the free traders." Parson Honeycombe rose, tower-ing over the detective, and gripped the handle of the teapot. "Do have some more tea, Mr. Adkins. I fancy there may be a little smuggling around these parts—yes, and in many other parts of England and Wales *and* Scotland."

"It is wrong, is it not? An offence against the State?"

"An offence against the State, certainly. But an offence against God, against mankind? I do not know. People are people, Mr. Adkins. We are all miserable sinners, so say the scriptures. It is my office in life, Mr. Adkins, to bring people to God, and if I cannot bring them to the State as well—have I failed so much in my task?"

The thieftaker noted that the parson had a deep, sonorous voice that matched his bulk and athletic frame, and that as he spoke he could have a fascinating—even a mesmeric—effect on the listener. This man could be more than a village cleric. He could be a true leader of men, for good—and maybe for evil. He could be feared as well as respected. If the man Bar-tholomew were odd, then so also was Honeycombe.

"You know your profession better than I, Mr. Honeycombe."

"I hope I do, Mr. Adkins. I am aware, for instance, that my first duty is that of saving souls. But I know also that there are they who do not sleep easily in their beds for thoughts of the French Bonaparte landing on our soil. They do not lose so much sleep over the free traders, who do no harm if they are not molested, and if there are arms to spare I would not hesitate to use them against an invading enemy."

To just what extent would this man be willing to use a weapon? Adkins kept the thought to himself.

"Well spoken, sir," he said. "But to a different topic. Might I ask after your daughter? She is in good health, I pray?"

"She would seem to bloom like the rose, Mr. Adkins, I am happy to say. She is also still grateful for the service you did her. I shall have her in to entertain you while I see if that Bartholomew is about." With the words the parson left the room, returning with Susannah, when Adkins sprang to his feet, bowing.

Parson Honeycombe left the drawing-room, and suddenly Adkins had forgotten the vicar and Bartholomew and the murders. It was as though a silken veil had been drawn across the dark association with evil that was inseparable from his daily life. Here was a moment of delight, just looking at her face, not yet finding his voice, and wondering why this should be so with a man who was never short of words.

It was Susannah who spoke first. "It is nice to see you, sir, for you did me a service and I assure you it is not forgotten."

"I—I was happy so to do, Miss Honeycombe." *In the name of God, there was something strange in this woman's smile, some quality in her eyes he had never seen before in any living soul.* It was the sort of moment when a painter gazes at a face or scene for the first time and longs to capture its beauty on canvas.

There were tales about her, too. God, why were there tales about everyone here?

"Do you plan to stay in these parts for long, Mr. Adkins?"

"I am enjoying my stay."

"Are you *quite* sure, sir?"

"Quite. Why do you ask?"

"I—just wondered."

"Oh."

She opened her mouth to speak, closed it again without a murmur and her eyes fell.

Adkins, a brave man in most circumstances, forced himself to ask a question. "Pray do not think it forward of me, Miss Honeycombe, but I have brought with me an exceedingly fast curricle from London. I—I wondered if you would care to take a ride with me some time. The countryside is at its best, and I assure you that a ride in this, the latest of its type, would be most entertaining."

"I should love to, Mr. Adkins, but I am afraid I might not be so free to accept your offer as you might think."

"I see," said Adkins, not seeing.

"There is, you see, someone who might not care for it. Do not ask me why."

"There is, perhaps—another gentleman?"

"I should prefer not to say. But do not take it amiss, for Mr. Adkins I like you well and I am indebted to you. It is for that reason that I would risk giving you a warning."

There was a momentary light in her eyes, and the thieftaker thought it one of fear as, after the shortest pause, she spoke again and hurriedly. "Please let me tell you—and before my father returns—that I think you are in the greatest peril and that you should return to London this instant."

"I could not think of so doing." Adkins was smiling.

Susannah Honeycombe gave him a long and searching look. The gleam faded from her eyes and her smile was gone. To Adkins she was still beautiful, though there were those who might have thought her but pert and pretty. At that moment, suddenly and inexplicably, she was at once desirable and un-attainable.

"My father may return at any moment. Quickly, sir, allow me to tell you why I think you should go, and I plead of you not to ask me any questions," she said, and there was a new look in her eyes that was neither fear nor urgency nor panic—a look that in the days to come was to haunt the memory of the man from Bow Street.

"I know who you are, sir," she said, in a low, tense voice, "and precisely why you are here."

CHAPTER FOURTEEN

PARSON HONEYCOMBE brought Bartholomew Barley to the vicarage. They entered the drawing-room to a silence of ticking clocks, the visitor from London standing very stiffly, staring at the cleric's daughter, and she with her glances all downwards to the pale-patterned carpet.

But now there was no need to find words, and Miss Honeycombe said in a low voice that it had been nice to see the visitor again. "If you will excuse me, I will leave you with my father," she added, "and a very good day to you, Mr. Adkins."

The detective bowed, speaking no word. His mind was confused, filled with doubts and half-sad thoughts. He was in no mood for an introduction to Bartholomew Barley.

He heard himself described by the vicar as "Mr. Adkins, who has taken quite a fancy to our village," and he replaced his hat and cane on the small table from which he had picked them up.

But Barley was shifting his weight from one foot to the other, looking distinctly uncomfortable, and Adkins's mind was at work again.

"Mr. Barley, I meet you at last," said the thieftaker. "What a difficult fellow you are to find."

Barley looked at the vicar, as if seeking permission to speak, received a calm gaze and a reassuring smile and said : "Pleased ter make yer acquaintance, I'm sure, and as to finding me, sir, it ain't always easy on account of I'm a seafarin' man."

"That, Barley, was not what I meant, but we will let the matter pass. Now—down to business."

"Wot business, sir?"

"Now, now, Barley, don't be alarmed," broke in Honeycombe. "Mr. Adkins would seem merely to be a—er, shall we say a student of human nature?"

"A—*wot*?"

"He is interested in people and the stories they have to tell of their adventures," explained the vicar.

"Oh."

"Barley, with your consent, I should like to meet you some time and talk of your experiences at sea. You *must* have some interesting tales to tell."

"Ordinary, sir. Ordinary."

"Well, maybe I could come to your home sometime. It is in Dymchurch, I take it?"

"Near enough. But no, please, not at 'ome. Er, wife's funny about strangers."

"Ah, well, we might meet in a tavern. Tonight, eh? What d'you say—*The Ship*, eight of the clock?"

Barley remained silent.

"I think it should be all right," said the vicar.

"Right then, sir. Eight o' the clock. But make it *The Ocean*. Beggin' yer pardon, vicar, can I go now?"

"Certainly, Barley," said Honeycombe. "But don't forget I should like to see you this afternoon."

As the door closed behind the seaman, the vicar smiled calmly. "When you talk to him, Mr. Adkins, take what he says with a pinch of snuff. He's a strange man."

"You are not, vicar, short of strange folk in these parts," smiled Adkins, taking his hat, gloves and cane and moving towards the door. "I should be delighted to pay you another visit while I am here."

"Any time, Mr. Adkins. My home is open to all."

Leaving the vicarage, the detective hurried down the road to his companion, reaching him as Barley, mounted on a horse, was fast disappearing down the high street.

"After him, captain," ordered Adkins. "He does not know

your face. Report to me where he goes. You'll find me at *The Ocean* in the village."

Elias's whip flicked and the curricle moved off.

The detective took lunch at *The Ocean Inn*, thinking deeply as he ate. That man Barley, his voice was somehow familiar, as though he had heard it before. Well, give it time and he may remember. . . .

Then there was Susannah Honeycombe. Hell and damnation, why should *she* appear to be involved in some mystery? Her of all people, her and her smile . . . and her eyes that held, as he did not yet know, the sadness of human life.

Who had told her who he was, and why he was there? In what way was she connected with the events that brought him there? Why could she not accept his company for a ride in the Kent countryside?

God, how the girl worried him. He kept seeing her face in his mind's eye, and her dainty, firm-breasted figure and her every graceful movement. Had he not enough to worry him without her? If only he could put her out of his mind for a time. . . .

His meal lay heavy in his belly, and he sought out the landlord and told him that if a man inquired for him he was to await his return. Then he went out and took to walking briskly, not an exercise he was accustomed to when he was his own calm man.

He walked down the high street and out on to the country road, the wind cooling his face and easing his thoughts.

Eventually he wasn't thinking at all, for he was aware only of the sights and sounds of the countryside. He turned and made his way back to *The Ocean*.

The curricle was drawn up outside, and Elias was to be found in the taproom. The captain was eager to talk, but Adkins silenced him with a raised finger. "Not here," he said. "A spin in the curricle, eh?"

"I followed your man," said Elias, as they drove up the high street. "He called at a cottage not a mile out of the village, and I should fancy that is where he lives. We're driving that way now and I'll show you the place as we pass. Then he mounted again and rode on further out, calling at an inn standing all by itself on the coast and called *The Floating Light*. He stayed there only a few minutes."

"Long enough to leave a message, eh?" inquired Adkins.

"Just about that, I'd say. Then he rode back to the cottage. I made inquiries where the inn is. It's near a spot known as St. Mary's Bay, less than a couple of miles from Dymchurch."

"Good, captain. We'll pay a call on *The Floating Light*."

"Aye, sir."

When they had driven a little further, Elias hauled the horses to a standstill. "The cottage," he said, pointing.

The little building sat in a solitude of scrubland between the road and the beach. Even in the afternoon sunlight it lay dejected and forlorn, like a place where no one lived—or wanted to live. It was a habitation rather than a home. Its last coat of white-wash had long peeled and discoloured. If Barley were the man Adkins thought he was, then the cottage might have for him but two advantages: few passers-by would give it a second glance, and it was near enough to cliffs honeycombed with caves where a man might hide out if the need arose.

"Drive on," said the detective. "The sight of the place depresses me."

Half a mile brought them within sight of *The Floating Light*. As their carriage rounded the bends and climbed the hills, the inn seemed from a distance to ride the rolling moors, high above the washing sea, like a wreck that would not sink. It had been built, for some reason beyond the ken of man, full in the path of every land-flung gale. At night the lamp above its dark oak door would be the only light to be seen for miles.

The sea-wind blew directly at this door, and at a touch of the latch it slammed inwards, raising the echoes.

The landlord came forward, fat and paunchy, wiping his

hands on his apron, and his smile was large and welcoming. "Good day, good sirs," he said in tones that matched his jovial face. "What may I do for you?"

"You may set before us a tankard of your best," said Adkins, "and I shall buy for yourself whatever is your pleasure."

It was not long before landlord and visitors were on the best of terms, and the thieftaker, once more thanking alcohol for its uses in business, announced that he knew one of the man's customers.

"Who be that, then?"

"Bartholomew Barley."

"Oh, Bart. I knows Bart."

"Pleasant fellow," said Adkins.

"Aye." The landlord did not seem altogether convinced of the statement. "Aye, some say so."

"You do not seem so sure."

"Well, there's some as thinks he's got a bit above 'imself since 'e rose in the world."

"Oh?" The expression invited further elucidation.

"Aye. Once 'e were an or'nary seaman. But now 'e's skipper o' the *Kentish Maid*, an' a fine new lugger she is. Talks as though 'e owns 'er. Owns 'er, my arse."

"Is there some doubt?"

"There's some as doubts it, and afraid to say so to 'is face. Nasty bit o' work is that Bart, if you was to ask me. 'Orrible and 'ateful, that's wot I'd call 'im, and I ain't afraid to say so. Kick 'im in the cods I would—beggin' yer pardon, gents—soon as look at 'im. If 'e pays 'is pint, 'e can have it, and that's the best I can say, sirs."

"Must say, don't know him that well myself," explained Adkins. "Mere acquaintance. Tell me, landlord, does he come here to meet anyone—anyone special?"

"Comes ter meet 'is saucy little whore, her my servin' wench and 'im a married man. Disgustin', that's wot I calls it. Called not an hour agone ter leave word 'ed see 'er tonight at nine. Randy bastard!"

" 'Tis not against the law, I suppose, but does he meet anyone else here, eh?"

"Seen 'im come more'n once to meet a big gen'leman. Most tall, sir. Bart's no little 'un, but this gen'leman—well, 'e's a bloody giant compared. Strange voice, most deep, sir, and as though 'e's talkin' queer. Don't talk to no one till Bart slinks in."

"Do they meet often here?"

"Seldom, sir."

"Do you know the gentleman?"

"Wouldn't know 'im if 'e were to walk in this minute. All muffled up, 'e is. Big scarf 'iding 'is physog. All I knows is 'e 'as the voice o' a gen'leman. Now, gents, will ye take a drink along o' me?"

Driving the windy road back to Dymchurch, the insuperable Adkins had quite recovered his high spirits. "Damned useful conversation, that," he declared. "If that Bart isn't head over heels in this business, I'll eat my topper, brim first."

"Don't like the sound of him myself," said Elias. "Wager you'll take him for murder."

"I might do that," said the thieftaker. "It could well be his hand that fired the pistol, for we know he was at the windmill that night. But there's more in this than murder, and I'm going to take it easy until I know more about the whole matter. Now there's something I'd like you to do for me. I'd like you to become a regular customer at *The Floating Light*, and take stock of that Mr. Adams if he should arrive. You might get something out of Bart's whore-piece as well. You could start tonight, for I'm to meet our mutual friend Bart. A ship's captain, eh? Most interesting."

* * *

Bartholomew Barley was most uncommunicative. "Well, I've 'ad adventures, o' course. Sea's a funny thing, Mr. Adkins."

"Where do you sail to, skipper?"

" 'Ere and there."

"Anywhere—in particular?"

"Round the coast. English ports."

"To other countries?"

" 'Olland. 'Olland's with us in the war, on our side, so to speak."

"Any other country you put in to?"

"No."

"France?"

"No."

"Not France."

"No."

"They do say some captains still trade with France."

"I told yer. Not France. There's a bloody war on, ain't there?"

"Of course there is. Fancy my forgetting. But about the yarns you must have to tell. Have you ever been shipwrecked?"

"Can't say I 'ave."

"Wager you've ridden a storm or two, skipper."

"Aye."

"Are you sailing soon?"

"Don't know."

Adkins bought more ale. "Got an idea, Captain Barley," he said, suddenly. "Will you take me on your next voyage? Promise to be as good as gold and do anything you say."

"Never take no strangers."

"Not even if I pay?"

"Not if you was to give me an 'undred."

"Ah, Mr. Barley, you've got me there, for I can't afford a hundred. Another tankard, eh? Or a tot of geneva?"

It was as Bart rose to go that a realization struck Adkins with such force that he banged his tankard down on the table but retained an inscrutable expression.

The man's voice! At the vicarage he had fancied he had heard it before. Now he remembered.

It was the voice that had come to him from the dark interior of the old windmill just before he had been knocked senseless from behind.

*   *   *

The skipper had left Adkins at the earliest opportunity, spitting in disgust as he put his foot to the stirrup. For he had been informed specifically of the true identity of Mr. Adkins and cautioned accordingly.

"Get nuthin' out o' me," the seaman said to himself, "not in 'ell 'e won't." *One silly prodnose sent from Bow Street, against a gang such as theirs, and him a little toff all dressed up like a lord and as polite as may be—why, he, Bart Barley, could lift him up with one hand whenever the time came and throw him over a cliff top into the sea.*

Besides, Bart had money now, little linen bags of it hidden away in his cottage, and he knew one way to spend it, the way he would spend it now. That fornicating wench at *The Floating Light*. Sarah Sandals. She'd do the necessary any time you liked, for a silver coin or two.

When he presented himself in the doorway of the inn, she was there sitting on a love-settle, drinking gin that another had bought for her, and he a man who kept a carbine, a cutlass and a pair of pistols in the boot of a curricle drawn up behind the inn—not that Bart knew that, of course. And this man a stranger, as big as himself, with a jaw that jutted and a steady gaze. Just an ordinary stranger, of course, not dolled up like that pimping little fancy man from Bow Street.

"Hey you!" barked Bart. "Get to 'ell out o' that seat. Wot d'yer think you're doin', Sary? S'posed ter be awaiting fer me, you wanton little tart."

"And wasn't I?" retorted Sarah Sandals, pertly. "I'm 'ere, aren't I, clevershins?"

"Well, you there," growled Bart. "Shift outer that seat."

"Are you speaking to me?" inquired Elias, calmly.

"Yus."

"Well don't—else your manners improve somewhat. I shall make way if the lady wishes it, not you."

"Better go, sweetie," cooed Sarah, nudging Elias.

Elias rose unhurriedly from the seat, slowly drawing himself to his full height and bringing his eyes to the level of Barley's, not a foot away. When the seaman had lowered his gaze, the policeman picked up his tankard and moved to another table.

Bart sat down beside Sarah, plying her with drink, his arm around her waist and his fingers fumbling, kissing her neck and repeatedly asking a question. "Come to the barn, Sary, my sweet?"

"Cross the lady's hand with silver, then," giggled the wench.

Three times he asked and three times he handed her a silver piece. On each occasion she dropped the coin into the top of her bodice. When at last it appeared that her price had been paid, the pair moved out through the back door.

The landlord came to Elias's table and sat down. "There she goes, the hussy, and him wed to another this many a year," he said. "But bain't my business, I s'pose, and so long as they don't do aught unseemly before my customers. Like to see Bart's arse kicked, that I would, though."

"You don't like him?"

"I 'ates 'im."

"Well, keep your eyes and ears open, and maybe we can get your gallivanting skipper into some trouble before he's finished."

"Meaning?"

"Meaning nothing, save that I don't like him either."

"Well, if you can get 'im brought down a peg, do it whenever you can, my friend, and I'm the man to help you."

Some time later, Bart and Sarah returned, the former brushing straw from his clothes and the woman with her dress crumpled and tying the laces of her bodice.

She took her seat again on the settle, while the seaman ordered ale, drained the tankard in one and left.

"Excuse me, landlord, while I talk to the lady again," Elias said to the innkeeper.

"Pah!" exclaimed the landlord. "All the same ye are with a pint or two of liquor inside o' you. Bed anything with a pair o' tits you would."

"Don't jump to conclusions, my friend," observed the policeman. "I just want to *talk* to her."

Elias rose and sat down beside Sarah. "Come back to me, eh, dearie?" she greeted him.

"Aye. Tell me, are you that man's sweetheart?"

"Sweetheart? Don't make me laugh."

"You like him, though."

"All I likes is 'is money."

"You wouldn't lift a finger to help him then if he were in trouble?"

"Not me."

Elias put his hand in his pocket. "Can you keep a secret from him?"

" 'Course I can."

Elias took her hand and placed a silver coin in it. "That's just for keeping a secret then."

"Oh, so you wants it, then, too?"

"Want what?"

"*It.*"

"Oh no. As a matter of fact, no."

"You gives me money and you don't want it?" gasped the astonished woman.

"I just want you to talk, and if you do there's more money where that came from."

"Gawd," observed Sarah. "Thought I knew men. Thought you was all the same. Wot do you want to know?"

"Well, me dear, I just wanted to know if he'd told you anything."

"Anythin' like wot?"

"Like about his job as a ship's captain."

"Wot's it worth?"

"Nothing if you tell him."

"I shan't tell."

Elias put another coin on the table. "Well, you could earn that, too."

"Will if I can. 'Tis much easier way o' making money than goin' out to the barn. Wot d'yer want to know?"

"When he sails, what cargo does he deal in?"

" 'E don't tell me that. Only thing he told me just now is that he sails not tomorrow night but the night after."

Elias raised his voice. "Landlord, another gin for the lady— a big 'un."

When Sarah had tossed back the gin Elias gave her a third coin. "Where is he sailing to?"

The woman put her hand to her mouth to stifle a hiccup. She was getting distinctly the worse for the alcohol she had consumed. "Promised ter bring me back some lace," she slurred. " 'E's sailing to France."

CHAPTER FIFTEEN

"So he puts out the night after tomorrow," mused Adkins, crashing a fist into his palm, "and it *is* to France he sails, and at night, eh? Just the shady customer to do business in the dark."

He clapped Elias on the shoulder. "Excellent, my friend! Truly excellent! You have done well. Exceeding well. Did you know there is a vacancy for another Runner at Bow Street? Would you care for the job?"

"Maybe. But who's to say I'd get the promotion?" The captain, patrolling the streets of London, had learned caution. If he were elevated to the rank of thieftaker he would have to learn patience, too. "What qualities would I need for the job, sir?"

"Just two—the first to have your wits about you, the second never to rely on guesses but on knowledge of the facts instead. Keep up your good work, my friend, and I might have a word in Sir Richard's ear. It's up to him, of course, and I dare not make a promise. As a captain you now get five shillings a night, do you not?"

"I do."

"Well, if you *did* have the good fortune to become a thief-taker, why—you'd make a fortune compared with that."

"The way you talk of a thieftaker's work, it sounds easy," said Elias, "but we all know it is not."

"Nothing's simple that's worth while, and nothing's easy that makes a bag of gold. Reckon the Runners do earn their fees and expenses." Suddenly Adkins was on his feet. "Now I'll tell you what I'd like you to do, friend. For the next two days and more, haunt that inn as though you were a ghost. Already we seem to have made an ally of the landlord. Make him now as your own brother. Become most friendly with him."

"Aye, sir."

"And with that Sarah Sandals."

"Aye, sir."

"But not too friendly." Adkins dug his companion in the ribs. "You don't want the pox."

"Don't worry," said the captain, grinning. "She's a proper blowse, that one. Wouldn't drink out o' the same glass as her, let alone——"

"Right then. I shall take over some inquiries in Dover, where the Frenchman was murdered. Tonight we shall stay here at *The Ocean*. Tomorrow you can drive me to the inn at Folkestone, where I'll borrow a nag—I'd never handle the curricle—and then you can return the next day and put your nose to the ground at *The Floating Light*.

When the two had parted company the next day at the *Oddfellows' Arms* Adkins went to his room and lay sprawled for a time puffing at a clay pipe.

His thoughts floated like the tobacco smoke. The three Frenchmen had no doubt been murdered by order from France. How had that order come? Bartholomew Barley, who sailed his ship to France, could be the link. But only a link. Barley, by the very nature of him, was no genius.

Who had killed the midshipman? Well, that could be Barley, too. He had been seen walking towards the old windmill. But Barley, skipper of a lugger though he may be, was a man who did as he was told.

Who, then, was the genius? Hackett? No. It would take that man all his time to run his tavern and tell tales. Of all the strange folk on this benighted coast, Honeycombe was the strangest. The thieftaker could trust all he had met—aye, and including Bart—more than he could that big, raw-boned, deep-voiced cleric. Come to that, was he a real parson? Or an imposter?

He took quill and paper, addressed a letter to his colleague John Clark at Bow Street, and put it on the mail coach for London. It read:

My dear friend John,

This by my hand is writ in the hope that your own inquiries in London are prospering. For I am not for my parte making as much headway as I would wish.

This Letter is also to ask of you a favour, for I have met up with a moste ill-assorted Reverend Gentleman in these partes by the name of Honeycombe. I have already ascertained that he calls himself, in full, John Wyndham Honeycombe, and that he has had the living at Dymchurch in Kent for the past seven years. I am so suspicious of this Reverend Gentleman that I would ask the favour of you, busy as I know you are your goode self. Could you please, however, put your nose into the Records of Clergymen in the citie and find out for me if this gentleman is indeed a priest and has been properly ordained?

Please send your reply by mail to me at The Oddfellows' Arms at Folkestone.

I shall buy you on my return a large glass of your favourite tipple in lieu of thanks.

Yours,

Harry Adkins.

*   *   *

The despatch of the letter, Adkins felt, could open up a whole new line of inquiry, and for some hours his movements belied his usual apathetic demeanour.

In the yard he snapped his fingers impatiently. "A horse, fellow, this instant," he called to a groom. "I've Mr. Barker's say-so, and put the loan of it down to my account."

He did not altogether enjoy the journey to Dungeness, for it was many miles and he was not the man to relish a bouncing ride on a mount he urged to give of its best.

But his eyes were sparkling as he burst in through the door

of the watch house. "Lieutenant," he said to Hogan, dispensing with the formalities, "what do you know of the *Kentish Maid*?"

"A two-masted lugger on the coastal trade," replied Hogan. "Spotted her often passing the point."

"Ever been suspicious of her?"

"No."

"Well, *I* am. Damned suspicious."

"D'you want her searched?"

"In the name of God, no. That would spoil everything. Listen carefully, she's skippered by a man named Barley, as ugly a brute as ever you saw, and what's more—she sails to France."

"The devil she does."

"Will you do me a favour, lieutenant?"

"I have told you, Mr. Adkins. I shall help all I can."

"Excellent! Find out all you can about her, but do not interfere with her. She takes the night tide tomorrow. Can you have a ship trail her without her suspecting for a moment that she is followed?"

"Shouldn't be too difficult."

"Excellent fellow. Let us just see where she sails. But remember—do not interfere with her."

Adkins was mounted again, not waiting for a reply, and riding as hard, and as uncomfortably, back to Folkestone.

Here he renewed his acquaintanceship with Mr. Customer Fordingham, who spilled snuff down his embroidered waistcoat in astonishment at this brisk, new personality whom he scarcely recognized as he who had languorously interviewed him in the past.

"The murdered Frenchman at Dover." Adkins shot the words at him.

"Ye-es."

"Do you know anything about him?"

"Only that—he was a Frenchman and had fled here to escape the guillotine."

"Precisely. Did you ever make his acquaintance?"

"Never."

"Do you know anyone who did?"

"No."

"Did you know he was in the habit of—er, visiting France?"

"I did not. I never saw his name on any passenger list."

"I am not surprised. I should think he used more than one name. If you hear anything about him—or of anyone who might have inquired of him—please to send a message to me at the soonest. You know where to find me."

"I'm at your service, Mr. Adkins."

"Now to something else. I suspect the *Kentish Maid* of being a smuggler. Anything you hear about her give me word without delay. But for the time being let her come and go without hindrance. Do not on any account have her searched."

Fordingham rose, his face reddening. "A moment, Mr. Adkins," he said, raising his voice, "who do you think you are to give me orders?"

The thieftaker rose, too, returning the customs chief's gaze. "I am an ordinary citizen of this country," he said. "But I am also an officer from Bow Street, and I am engaged at this moment on a matter of national importance. I speak not with my own authority, but with that of Sir Richard Ford."

"Mr. Adkins, *you* are here to find a murderer and not, if I may say so, doing it with the greatest despatch. If I wish to detain the *Kentish Maid* I will do so."

"You will do no such thing."

"Mr. Adkins, might I remind you that you are here at my request and that I am retaining your services. Pray do not give me orders. Otherwise I might dispense with your services."

"That you may do whenever you please, sir. But I must inform you that my services are now retained also by the Secretary for War, and it is on *his* authority, and not my own, that I now address you. I would not wish to have to report you to *him*. Mr. Fordingham, if you had but waited I would have told you before you got yourself into such a pother that we are now dealing with something more than murder."

"Oh? Of what are we dealing?"

"We are dealing with matters of national security."

"Have I your word for it, Mr. Adkins?"

"You have. Now have I *your* word that you will not detain the *Kentish Maid*? I ask it of you *only for the time being*."

"All right, Mr. Adkins. You have my word."

"Thank you. I will explain more to you later, for at the moment I have much to do. What I can say, however, is that if I be successful in the matters now to hand you may well end up with less smuggling on your hands than you have had for years."

Fordingham forced a smile. "That would please me greatly," he said. "I am afraid I will have to trust you."

"I am afraid you will. Good day to you, Mr. Fordingham." At the door he paused. "Have I still the use of your stable room should I require it?"

"Most certainly you have, Mr. Adkins. It is at your disposal whenever you should wish it."

The detective then posted to Dover, where he checked with every inn as to its residents on the night before the murder. But he heard no word of anyone remotely resembling the stranger who had taken the coach for London shortly after the shooting of M. Rohan-Marichal.

*　　*　　*

Glancing neither to left nor right, the man who called himself Adams entered *The Floating Light* on the night the *Kentish Maid* was to sail, and strode heavily to the table furthest from the lamp's glow. As always, his muffled figure intrigued the inn's clientele. For no reason, they stared, hitched their smocks, studied their boots and took longer pulls at their beer. Momentarily, the river of their talk was dammed.

In the silence the newcomer's weight on the rickety chair caused creaks and sounded like the groans of dying men.

Before he reached the table one figure had extracted itself from the cluster round the fire and taken a seat at a table in another dark corner.

Had the stranger entered in a more friendly and less imperious manner, he would have seen this figure as a man apart from the rustics. He might also have noted the landlord nudging the man, or heard the hiss of the whispered words : "That's 'im."

As it was, when the newcomer looked up the landlord wore his usual expansive smile and guffaws were greeting the end of a tale that some worthy had been recounting.

The innkeeper approached Adams. "A good 'e'en to you, sir," he said, cheerfully.

Adams grunted.

"What may your pleasure be?" inquired the landlord.

"Ale," came the reply in a low, deep voice, and the economy of speech made it difficult for Richard Elias, straining his ears from the other far corner, to decide whether he had heard the voice before.

It was not long before Bartholomew Barley opened the door, closing it carefully and walking somewhat furtively across the room, stooping to avoid the lamp hanging from the low-ceilinged room.

"If it ain't the skipper 'imself," sang out the landlord, his geniality tinged with sarcasm.

Barley pushed past him and joined the tall figure in the shadows.

The innkeeper followed him to the table.

"Flog off," bullied Barley, "and come when you're called. Wait a minute. Fetch me ale."

The landlord brought him a tankard, and received payment but no thanks.

Strain as he would Elias could hear nothing of the conversation, for there were several long trestle tables between them, and the two had their heads close together and they spoke in undertones.

But there was one thing that Elias was able to note, and it was an action about which he would tell Harry Adkins at the first opportunity. For it was done discreetly and carefully—and after a furtive glance at the fireside throng. Something white and crisp was handed from the tall stranger to the swaggering sea captain, and if it was not a letter then the police captain's eyes were seriously deceiving him.

CHAPTER SIXTEEN

THE *Kentish Maid* sailed with the night tide. She slipped away quietly, with no barking of orders, Barley himself at the helm and his crew working in a silence to which they were well used.

She was no more than a moving shadow in the dark, a ghost ship with no human sounds aboard . . . only the slap of the drooping sails as she waited for a fair wind to fill them, rolling and dipping in the lee of the sky-high cliffs, lonely in the lapping tide.

The vessel was not, however, to be as companionless as her skipper wished her to be. Before the night had invaded her anchorage a naval sloop had twice passed close to her port bow, the captain hailing her cheerfully by megaphone.

"Ahoy there, skipper! A fair wind and a good tide."

"Aye, a good night," Barley had yelled in return.

"Sailing before dawn?"

"Mebbe. Mebbe not."

It was a good night for sailing. Now the *Kentish Maid* was clear of her haven, out in the wind's whip and the sea's heave. Her sails bellied and the masts took the strain. Her timbers creaked as she ploughed perfectly into the rollers that were her proper home, the eternal, restless ocean for which she had been built . . . her own element, her elder, embracing sister—and sometimes her master.

Barley coughed and spat deftly between two spokes of the wheel. Who said she was not his ship? She was his now, anyway, out on the night sea, in which pray God his skills would always win.

The sloop lay hidden in a cove up coast until Barley's riding light, dipping and glowing and winking in the far, dark distance, was in danger of blinking right out. Then, and only then, did the naval captain give the order to sail out far in the smuggler's wake, nodding to his first officer, who had already been primed to keep that moving light ahead constantly within the range of his telescope.

On went the smuggler, her salt-encrusted bows cleaving the mid-channel plain, her spray-drenched figurehead, a dark-oak, naked maiden with gleaming-wet breasts and streaming, carved-wood hair, rising and plunging like an ancient flying goddess.

No moon, no stars lit her lonely, watery path. With the heavens black above him, Bartholomew Barley, who was a good seaman if nothing else, sailed this night half by instinct and half by dead reckoning. The wind changed, and for a time he had to tack. Then the breezes veered in his favour again, and the sails were re-trimmed and the vessel forged ahead again. Barley wiped salt spray from his mouth and with his harsh, deep voice added an old, old shanty to the gratings and crashings of his vessel and the uncomprehendable song of the sea.

This was what he loved best, sailing his beautiful little sea maid, pitting his skills against the changing, changeless waters, this and going a-whoring and getting sodden drunk on Kentish ale. For he was no better than need be and no saintlier than all the poor mortals of this strange and striving world. And but for a certain dubious crime he had committed against the laws of earthbound man, and the hold that this devilish Adams had on him because of it, he would have sailed and fornicated and taken his little bite at smuggling—and nothing more. But Bartholomew Barley was caught in the web.

Behind him the naval sloop came on. Better fitted, fuller rigged, possessing more and better instruments, she kept her distance with inexorable perfection.

"She's making sou'-sou'-west, Mister Mate," the sloop's

commander said to his first officer. " 'Tis France or Spain, and no doubt on it."

"Then he's a traitor, sir," declared the younger officer.

"Well, unpatriotic, at least," said the captain.

When the smuggler put in to Roscoff the sloop stood off far out to sea. Because her orders were to watch and wait and stay unseen, her captain could not be precisely sure which French port the *Kentish Maid* had entered. But enter one she had.

The naval commander brought his ship about. Then the lone vessel lay but a few leagues from enemy soil, but no man of her crew voiced the prayer that they would not be sighted by a hostile flotilla.

To and fro patrolled the sloop, out of sight of the French coast, waiting. . . .

When the *Kentish Maid* was tied up, Barley left his crew aboard and made his way along the sleezy, windy shore street of the little port to the house where he would find the tall, greying Frenchman who made him so welcome.

On the way a woman dressed in cheap but stylish clothes detached herself from the shadows and accosted him. She had a flashing glance, but her eyes were red-rimmed and her face had the pallor of uncooked dough.

She spoke first in French, which Barley did not understand, though he was quite well aware of what she wanted.

"*Anglais.* Eengleesh sailor," she said then. "*Jig-a-jig. Le lit*— bed. *Vous-et-moi.* Eengleesh shilling, *oui*?"

Cocking a snook at her, he pushed her out of his way, growling a derisive phrase, of which the one word "pox" she understood, and spat after him as he continued on his way.

"Boussant will have better than that to offer," he said to himself, smiling.

He rapped on the door where he would find the French officer, but stepped smartly to one side as, glancing upwards, he saw a woman at an open window above him with a chamber pot in her hand. He was just in time, for the next instant the contents of the vessel spattered on the cobbles at his feet.

The door was opened by a burly soldier, Boussant's personal servant, and slowly and laboriously Barley pronounced the password that he had been taught : *"La-bas le Bastille."*

"Entrez," said the soldier.

Barley was taken then to a room where Napoleon's distinguished master spy, Colonel Jean-Paul Boussant, sat at a table studying a map.

His smile was a mere curve of the lips, his words clipped, but his voice pleasant.

"M'sieur Barley, take a seat. You are most welcome."

The smuggler's captain unfastened his shirt and took a letter from a linen wallet attached to a cloth belt he wore round his middle next to his skin.

"Ah, you have something for me?" said the French officer.

"Aye, this," replied Barley, handing him the letter.

Leaning back in his chair, Boussant idly tapped the edge of the envelope on the table. "One question, m'sieur, do you know who wrote this letter?"

"All I know, sir, is that it was not writ by the gentleman wot put it in my charge? Do yer want to know 'is name?"

"It is not necessary," said Boussant, smiling. "I only wished to know if you knew the writer, for it is in my interest that you do not. The fewer who know the identity of my correspondent the better it pleases me. You may understand my meaning?"

"Aye. I thinks I do."

The Frenchman used an evilly sharp dagger which lay on the table to open the envelope, and this is what he read:

> *Q01 to A01.*
> *All three fishermen who put out their nets at your end now dead. Their haul died with them.*
> *Regarding Co. information, as fisherman myself, am engaged now finding for you those parts of this coast where least fish abound, and therefore best parts for you to direct your fishing fleet. I may say now that some parts of coast facing you are most desirable as scarce any live at them nor*

are men set there to interfere with your fishing plans. **Full
information later.**

*Regarding movement in Ch., this more difficult, as un-
official ships have joined forces with official ones to guard
fishing grounds, and numbers of former not easy to assess
as no proper list ever seems to have been drawn up.*

I have the honour to be, sir,

your obedient servant,

Q01.

"Do not fasten your shirt yet, M'sieur Barley," said Boussant,
picking up a quill from the table. "I will write a letter for you
to forward in the same way on your return."

For a few minutes the French officer scratched away on a
piece of paper, which he placed in a blank enevelope. This he
handed to Barley, who placed it in the linen wallet and re-
arranged his dress.

"And now, M'sieur Barley, have you money in gold?" the
Frenchman asked.

"Aye, sir."

"Then we will arrange a cargo for you tomorrow. In the
meantime, I have as usual arranged some entertainment for
you to show how welcome you are. I shall have you taken to
a house where there will be free wine laid out and women from
whom you and your crew can choose. First, bring your crew to
my door."

The English skipper and his crew soon found themselves in
a house several streets away from Boussant's headquarters. In
a tawdry, ill-lit room they poured wine and waited for the
prostitutes who were in the pay of the French intelligence
officer. "Keep the English smugglers sweetened," Napoleon
Bonaparte had said. "They are our only link across the
channel." Napoleon's man at Roscoff had everything arranged
to fulfil that order, and he was an officer who paid attention
to detail.

Trapped in the room was a macabre, ghostly atmosphere.

Drawn, patched curtains shunned the daylight. The walls were lined with couches, the fabric of which was worn and shiny. There was a disagreeable, intangible odour. The threadbare carpet bore old, dark stains. Such light as there was came from candles on the tables, and these could be nipped out at a stretch of the hand of a seaman more shy than his fellows.

The women were mustered quickly by soldiers under Boussant's command, paid in cash and thrust into the room. Here they began to dance round, blowing kisses, singing French songs of dubious moral tone and containing words of endearment, the meaning of which the English sailors had come to know by association with actions which in the past had accompanied their utterance. As they skipped about before their lecherous audience, they lifted high their skirts and with movements disguised as part of the dance allowed from time to time their breasts to become fully revealed in their loose bodices.

Suddenly one man, bolder than the rest, leapt forward, grasped one by the arm and drew her to one of the couches where he had been drinking wine.

One by one, the others made their choice, until all round the room there were many fumblings, giggles, whisperings and embraces. In the scant light of the few candles that still flickered a dress here and a stocking there lay on the floor beside spilled wine. . . .

The candles had long guttered when the men of the *Kentish Maid*, garrulous and lewd-mouthed, satiated with sex, spilled out of the hot and airless room and out into the street, breathing gulps of sea air, clutching as prizes bottles still full of liquor and intimate articles of feminine underwear, and making their way to the quay and their bunks.

There, gulping more wine, they indulged in a camaraderie of shared obscenity.

"My wench bedded well."

"Wench? Wench be damned, you ignorant bastard. *M'amselle* yer mean."

"Mine 'ad such long 'air on 'er 'ead it came right down to 'er rump."

"Mine 'ad legs wot went right up to 'er arse."

"Experts they was. Bet they was from Paris."

"Bet they was."

In the morning, not so merry, the crew helped to load brandy, tobacco and laces into their ship. And this time they sailed in daylight so that they would be standing off their little home cove in darkness.

A few leagues out they sighted a ship. She was a considerable distance away, and Barley, keeping happily on course, assumed her to be a French vessel. Even when she drew a little nearer the smuggler's skipper gave little thought to her, for she was still a long way off.

The commander of the British sloop shaded his eyes as he kept sight of the ship that sailed from the French coast. The first officer kept his telescope trained on her until he was able to recognize some distinguishing marks.

"Think it's her," he said.

"Make sure, Mister Mate," ordered the captain.

At last the telescope picked up the name, white against her dark oak bows.

"It is her," said the first officer. "The *Kentish Maid*, sir."

Veering away from the smuggler, clapping on full sail, the sloop made all speed for England.

CHAPTER SEVENTEEN

THE LITTLE FERRET allowed himself a gleam of hope that he was at last on the trail. Elias had told him of the letter that had been passed to Barley in the cliff-top inn on the night he was to sail for France, and he now felt reasonably sure that he had discovered the secret postal service used by the murderer of the three French *émigrés*.

But there was still so much that he did not know. . . . Who had shot the midshipman? Were all four crimes linked? And who was the master mind behind the smuggling gang that operated so blatantly in this corner of the Kentish coast?

The last question was the most intriguing of all, and he had a strange feeling, which he was careful not to trust altogether, that the answer to this one would be the key to the whole mystery.

The celebrated thieftaker, however, had not been given his nickname for nothing. He was content to make no move until his knowledge of the facts was greatly improved.

But one question above all others was in danger of clouding the vital clarity of his mind. How did the charming Susannah Honeycombe fit into the pattern? For fit into it she most certainly did.

How did *she* know his true identity? Who had told her? Above all, why had an unaccountable fear sprung to her eyes as she warned him to leave Kent?

He would have to be careful of his thoughts about her, for whenever his mind wandered back to her, as it did so often, he was not quite his own man. . . .

Trying not to think of her, waiting for the return of the *Kentish Maid*, he decided to pay another call on Ransome Quested, whose work as a riding officer was, like his own on this assignment, directed against the free traders.

He rode to Dymchurch, entered the apothecary's shop and inquired for Quested.

"He is in his room upstairs," explained one of the assistants.

"Perhaps, then, you can inform him that I am here and that I should like to see him," said the thieftaker. "My name is Adkins."

"There is a person with him, and such a one as I am afraid I cannot disturb him," was the reply.

"Then I shall wait," said Adkins.

"You may take a seat, sir, if you please. But I am afraid you may tire of waiting. The person who is with him usually stays a long time."

"I shall wait," said the detective, "as long as need be."

"You may please yourself, sir."

Adkins sat on a hard, wooden chair. He was well used to waiting, and often in less comfortable conditions. But even he was compelled at last to remark: "Whoever is with Mr. Quested is remaining a deuced long time, eh?"

"Always does. Sorry, sir."

At last the door leading to the stairs opened and a figure came forward into the shop. It was a female figure, dressed for riding in a high-crowned hat like a gentleman's topper but smaller and not so wide at the top as at the brim, a long velvet skirt and a cut-away coat with a velvet collar. The lady was very trim and beautiful. Susannah Honeycombe!

She was long-faced, flushed and, on closer inspection, perhaps a little agitated.

"Miss Honeycombe," declared Adkins at once. "Delighted."

"Mr. Adkins." There was not a hint of a smile as she made to sweep past him.

He barred her way, bowing. "My dear lady. Pray not to hasten away, for it is most agreeable to see you again."

"I am afraid, sir, I am obleeged to make haste," she said, a huskiness in her voice.

At this moment she was a young woman with a face older than her years. Could his unexpected presence have wrought such a change in her? God grant this was not so.

"Then I shall not delay you," he said, stepping aside. "I'd not think of it. But I should like to meet you again at some convenient time and place. Your servant, Miss Honeycombe."

"If you wish to call at the vicarage—sometime—I cannot prevent it, sir. My father keeps open house for all." With the words she was hurrying past him towards the street.

He stared at the door through which she had gone, holding his hat and cane limply, making a conscious effort to hold his head higher.

"I think you may go up now," the shop assistant was saying. "Mr. Quested said you were to be admitted to him whenever you should call."

Adkins did not at first hear the words, but now they were seeping into his consciousness. "Ah, yes—thank you," he murmured, turning to ascend the stairs.

At sight of the thieftaker, Quested's face puckered into a merry smile. "Come in, Mr. Adkins," he boomed cheerfully. "Do come in."

"Good day, Mr.——" Adkins stopped speaking abruptly, his eyes gazing incredulously at the couch. For on it lay an article of female underwear.

"What—is that?" asked the detective, pointing.

"Oh, that. It is—er, what you think it is."

"Mr. Quested, Miss Honeycombe has this instant left you."

"Oh yes, so she has, Mr. Adkins, and that—er, article of clothing belongs to her. She must have left it by mistake when she dressed."

"Miss Honeycombe, the *vicar's* daughter—she *undressed* in this room?"

"Why, yes."

"Am I to take it, sir, that you are conducting——"

"But *of course* you would not understand," interrupted the apothecary, with extraordinary calmness. "I am not conducting anything. That is to say, I am not conducting *an affair*."

"Then I assume I am permitted to ask what in heaven's name you *are* conducting with the lady?" The voice was raised, and there was an unfriendly edge to it. It was unusual for the visitor to lose his professional calm. But he had the most unusual feeling towards Susannah Honeycombe, and at this moment he was speaking not as a thieftaker but as a man with strong instincts that had been stirred suddenly and deeply.

"Calm yourself, my dear Mr. Adkins, lest I have to prescribe a herbal mixture for your blood-pressure. Pray be seated while I explain."

Adkins, struggling to gain a grip on himself, sat down. "I am but a stranger to Dymchurch, and it may be I have no right to an explanation touching upon—upon any matter which does not concern my business here."

"Why, Mr. Adkins, of course I shall explain. Firstly, sir, did you know that I am a painter?" Quested was pointing, and Adkins was following the line of his finger. In a corner of the office stood an easel. Beside it on the floor stood a canvas, its face towards the wall.

"You—paint?"

"I do portraits, and I am painting Miss Honeycombe. Why, she is my best model. Today she has done a sitting. This time I am painting her in the semi-nude. Very artistic. The most beautiful body in Dymchurch, eh, Mr. Adkins? Allow me to show you."

Quested walked to the canvas and set it on the easel. It was certainly a painting of Susannah Honeycombe, of her hair flowing free, her slim, shapely shoulders, her firm breasts, her stomach and then—a length of silken material draping her body below that.

Adkins rose and walked to the easel, gazing speechless at the painting.

"She undressed," he heard Quested saying, "but behind that screen."

"You have been privileged to see a very beautiful body," said Adkins, his voice calmer now.

"Through the eye of an artist," said Quested. "The eye of the artist, you understand."

The thieftaker was thoughtful and silent. If the assistants in this shop knew of the painting, they would not, he suspected, have kept their lips sealed. Perhaps this was the thing that had given her a name for being "a harum-scarum." It could be the reason also for tales having reached Lieutenant Hogan that Quested was lovesick for Susannah, for how such gossip could be twisted in the telling!

"Forgive me for being, perhaps, a little too curious," said Adkins.

"Tut, man, think nothing of it. Now about our mutual interest, for I take it that is what you have come to see me about?"

"It is. Tell me, in your duties as a riding officer have you seen any preparations for another run by the free traders?"

"I know nothing of a run at the moment. I have made my patrols most assiduously and seen nothing on the coast of any moment. The more runs there are the less I am held in esteem as a riding officer. I do not want another to take place so soon."

"I do."

"In the name of God, why?"

"Because I think I may learn something from it about the murderer."

"You are convinced, then, that it was a free trader who shot the midshipman?"

"I am. Accordingly, I should be pleased if you would warn me at the soonest of any sign of another run."

"You can count on me," declared Quested, his eyes flashing.

"The damned free traders, they are like a plague on this coast."

"They are certainly that. But I do not think we are dealing only with smugglers."

"Why not? They are most dreadful fellows, and the gangs are becoming as dangerous as ever they were."

"That is true. But I do not think they would go to Dover, knock on a man's door and shoot him dead when he opened it."

"Yes, I had heard of the murder at Dover. But somehow I feel that it is not my concern. Not in my parish, so to speak, as a riding officer."

"But the killing at the windmill, that is your concern, specially as it would appear to be connected with smuggling."

"I should say that one is very much my concern. But the one at Dover, I know nothing about it, and I am sorry it occurred, because it complicates the one that happened in my area. Do you think the two crimes are connected?"

"The possibility exists. It is not far to Dover."

"I hope they are not connected. It could make the matter more difficult for us regarding the midshipman's killer."

"You can never tell, Mr. Quested. It might make it easier."

"Well, you are more experienced in taking thieves and murderers than I. For my part, I am more concerned with discovering when a run is to take place and notifying the coast watch. But 'tis not easy. The smugglers are a damned canny lot, blast 'em." Quested rose from his desk. "Mr. Adkins, let us talk in more congenial surroundings. Would you care to dine with me at my home?"

"Delighted."

"Then we shall get off this minute, for I am damned peckish. Used to live here above the shop, but one of my assistants resides with his wife in the kitchen and in a room next to this study. Keeps an eye on the place at night-time."

Quested's home was a three-storeyed house where the Dymchurch high street became a leafy lane. It did not have the pretentions of a country house, but its frontage had been expensively covered with a new stucco plaster and it sat graciously beyond clipped hedges and a stretch of lawn and shrubbery, and its painted windows and door eyed the world with clean, white confidence. No large estate surrounded it, but there was a stable building, housing a carriage and a number of horses, and there was a manservant to open the door when the thud of the big brass knocker summoned him.

This man had neither the air nor the clothes of a footman, nor did Adkins expect him to have such, for no doubt Quested, successful apothecary though he was, would not number among the wealthiest in England.

When Adkins was presented to Quested's wife he found her a somewhat unlikely spouse for the tall, broad-shouldered and handsome riding officer. Her long dress, with its waist-line fashionably high under the arms, was of the most beautiful muslin, but she was too angular to be graceful.

Her black hair was worn frizzed and with a fringe on the forehead instead of being dressed in ringlets, and her nose was thin, large and slightly hooked. Seen by firelight or behind a guttering candle, her head might have been mistaken for that of a massive bird of prey.

But there was no ferocity in Sylvia Quested, for the huge, dark eyes, set in a face of faded agreeableness, were the saddest the detective had ever seen. It was as though something, sometime, had hurt her beyond forgetting.

She wore a white Norwich shawl, clipped high at the neck, as though to proclaim to the world an unassailable modesty.

In the dining room the walls had been re-panelled, much of the furniture was of the fashionable rosewood, and the chairs had expensive brass inlays. A glance told Adkins that the mead beakers and wineglasses were of the finest Venetian, that the candlesticks, plate, tankards and tea-pots were of solid silver—the latter no doubt for smugglers' tea, for even the innocent paid cheaply yet unknowingly for such goods.

"You have a fine house, sir." Adkins was beginning to think

that, in spite of his fees and emoluments, he might have done better to have gone into the apothecary business.

"I do tolerable well, Mr. Adkins. My business was well-established before ever I took it over. I am fully qualified in my profession, and folk come in to Dymchurch from miles around for my recipes."

"You would almost make me feel envious of you."

"Tut, Mr. Adkins, what are a few expensive baubles compared with your own interesting profession, and I suppose there are more in the entire heart of London who know your name than who are aware of mine in these parts."

The polite Adkins turned his attention to Mrs. Quested. "You will find this coast most popular in the summer months. Have you seen Royal Prinny's new place at Brighton?"

"I seldom leave the house, Mr. Adkins," she replied, her haunted eyes avoiding his glance.

"My wife does not enjoy good health," was Quested's explanation.

"I have much to occupy my time," was her own. "I make all our own beer and mead. I cook and bake and do a little needlework, and when the weather is warm I sit in the garden, which is made most private by the high hedges."

When Mrs. Quested had left the two at their port the thief-taker continued his discussion about the crimes he was investigating. "The smuggling gang is extensive hereabouts. Have you any idea of its numbers?"

"I could not hazard a guess," admitted the riding officer. "There must be folk taking some part or other in it whom neither you nor I would ever suspect."

Ransome Quested and Lieutenant Hogan, both with their forthright personalities, were good men to have on his side, thought Adkins. But he was not so sure about the local customs chief.

"What do you think of Fordingham?" he asked.

"I do not know rightly what to think of him."

"The thieftaker smiled wryly. "I will tell you what *I* think of him. I'd say he's either quite ineffectual or a very clever man who sometimes winks the eye at the free traders. He would seem to grow fat and lazy."

"I am inclined to agree with you, Mr. Adkins."

"Now I'd say that Bart Barley is up to no good," suggested Adkins.

"The man is a dolt. He has no brains."

"I'd agree on that. Who do you suppose, then, is the real leader of the gang, the master-mind so to speak?"

"Whoever he is, he hides himself away like an old fox. 'Tis certain I have never got within a mile of his lair. Have *you* any ideas on the matter?"

The detective sipped wine meditatively. "Well, my friend, there is a certain gentleman, and a strange one, in this parish, and I cannot make head nor tail of him. Vicar Honeycombe."

"Well, *you* said it, sir, not me. Far be it from me to say a word against a man of the cloth. I take it our conversation is of the most secret?"

"If it is not that, then we should not be collaborating."

"Then I shall come out with my true feelings, Mr. Adkins. He would appear to have too much truck with the smugglers. He knows that his congregation, his very choir, is full of free traders, yet he has never preached a single sermon against their activities. He is a man of God, yet he is prepared to kill with his own hands if the French invade our coast."

"Much of what you say I knew already," mused Adkins. "I wonder . . . I just wonder if he is the man I seek."

"As to that," said Quested, slowly, "I am a man of some devout feelings, and I cannot be brought to hound down a Clerk in Holy Orders. As to that, sir, you must find out for yourself."

CHAPTER EIGHTEEN

HARRY ADKINS RODE the downs like a Puritan parson brooding on the incalculable sin of man. A weight like gallow's gloom pressed down on his whole being, darkening his brow in the sunlight. He sat heavy in the saddle, his grip lying light as featherdown on the reins and the horse having its idle way of him, roaming as though quite riderless and cropping the grass at its own fancy.

Foremost in his mind lay the one leaden thought—*Pray God the vicar is not the man I seek.* It was a supplication to which he had no right, either as a peace officer or as an ordinary humble soul.

At this most private moment it was the real Harry Adkins. The supercilious man from Bow Street, the fashion-conscious dandy, the clear-brained searcher after truth, the slow-moving, inexorable hunter, the logical, quick-witted thieftaker—all these had blown away on the wind like scraps of fairy thistledown.

Oh, he was not worried for Honeycombe himself, for he did not much like the fellow, nor yet that he was a priest ordained under God's holy laws.

For the little detective would have the courage to take any man to his just reward, be he the highest in the land.

No, the reason for his prayer was that this big, booming, weatherbeaten cleric—if cleric he were, and this was now being set to the proof—was the father of a young lady named Susannah. Susannah, who dangerously filled his thoughts. Susannah, whose sad-sweet smile and changing ways had struck deeper into his being than the charms of any woman he had ever known—he, Harry Adkins, who had been no better than he need be with any willing wench. But Susannah must not be hurt. . . .

"God grant that he be not guilty." Suddenly he spoke the words aloud to the rolling downs and the marsh wind and the wheeling curlews, and they echoed in a great emptiness like a cry of pain in the half-way house between heaven and hell.

Yet he had not even the right to breathe his prayer for *her* sake. He had had but three meetings with her. On the first he had done her a service and she had thanked him prettily. On the second she had beseeched him, in effect, to get him gone and never to return. On the third she had passed him by with coldness on her lips.

Still less did he have the right to wish it as a thieftaker, for it did not accord well with his duty or with his techniques of logicality.

Rising within him was a dangerous conflict, and he had not thought it possible. . . . But Harry Adkins had not lived long enough to discover that the way of life was—undiscoverable.

A cool wind from France reached the white cliffs, bearing dark clouds to take the place of the lambs' wool that had fleeced snow in summer across the blue sky. Shadows passed over the downs and he did not see them. Squalls of rain gusted in from the sea, and he did not take his cape from the saddle bow to protect his best tan jacket.

For hours he did not know where he wandered. But suddenly he saw before him a black outline in the rain-dark distance. It was the windmill. The windmill where a young midshipman had been most brutally murdered. The sight of it brought him to a starker realization. The wind whipped cold rain in his face and stung his brain to new thought.

His hands tightened on the reins. The horse's dream sequence was over. Clumsily, for he was no active athlete, he wheeled the animal on to the hill path and put heels to its belly.

He was on his way to Dungeness and Lieutenant Hogan,

making decent haste on the windy heath, grim-faced and clear-eyed. And his jaw was jutting again.

He was unaware that another horseman, who had been shadowing him and had watched from the shelter of a copse, puzzled by the thieftaker's strange meanderings, now fell in behind him again at a very safe distance.

Hogan was taking the air at the doorway of the watch house, and Adkins did not pause to dismount. "Any news, lieutenant?" he called.

"Aye, sir. The *Kentish Maid*. She did go to France. Went into port. Remained a day and a night. Our ship made better sail and is home already. Your friend, Captain Barley, should be lying off shore later today."

"Thank you, lieutenant," said the thieftaker. "Remember, let her be. Allow her to land her contraband undisturbed, should she so wish. Believe me, my friend, it will suit my purpose the better."

The horseman who showed such interest in Adkins, again in hiding, was too far off to hear the words.

Waiting for neither reply nor promise, Adkins was off again, making for Folkestone and the *Oddfellows' Arms*—unaware that he was being most artfully followed.

* * *

The edge of day hung its strange silence over the cliffs. The rustling downs prepared for sleep. With the stealing shadows the birds went to their tree-top beds. The shutters were put up and soon *The Floating Light* would lose itself quietly in the dark, save for its one swinging lantern over the rock-girt porch.

Inside, by the crackling log fire, Richard Elias obeyed his orders and continued to haunt the place. "A good house you keep, landlord, and a decent jug of ale."

"There's none better round these 'ere parts," returned the innkeeper, benign with his visitor's constant praise.

"Suits me," said the police captain.

"And we," chorused a dozen smocked farm workers, raising their tankards.

During a lull in the conversation, one of the company, having spent his last coin, opened the door to depart. On the night wind came a distant thudding that became distinguishable as the sound of a horse being ridden hard.

The door closed on the echoes. But soon it was flung open, and a man entered with a wooden case under his arm. He asked for no refreshment, and by no one's leave took a fiddle from the case and drew the bow across the strings.

He played a simple air that had the sound of an old sea shanty, and the notes whined plaintively in the sudden silence.

An old man beside the fire quietly sang the words to it in a faded, croaky voice :

> *Oh, but ye've been long away*
> *Ye're welcome back again.*

One by one, nine of the inn's clientele laid down their tankards and left. The newcomer put away his violin, tucked the case under his arm and was gone.

He left a silence, the old man by the fire, two young farm labourers, the landlord and the policeman.

"Who was that?" asked Elias.

"Simon the fiddler."

"He plays a merry tune."

"Aye."

The occurrence was too odd to be left at that, and Elias rose, gripped his empty tankard and said to the landlord : "Come, another pint. I'll join you at the barrel and help you fill it, and whatever is your pleasure you must have at my expense. You're the best landlord I ever did see."

In the corner where the barrels stood the police captain put his mouth close to the innkeeper's ear. "What has just happened means something, or I'm a Dutchman. What does it mean?"

"Don't know as I dare say," whispered the landlord. "Got me livin' to think on."

"We're good friends," hissed Elias. "Swear I won't tell."

"I've a good mind to tell, most secret like. 'Tis summat I don't 'old with."

"Tell then."

" 'Tis the signal."

"What for?"

"For a run."

"The free traders?"

"Aye."

"When?"

"Tonight."

Elias drank his ale, making small talk but impatient to be off. Then he bade everyone a good night, and strolled leisurely to the door. At the other side of it he sprinted to the yard and leapt to the seat of the curricle. He was on the coast road, whipping the horses to a gallop, careering and rattling, racing for the *Oddfellows' Arms* at Folkestone with his news, and praying that he would be in time.

* * *

Two others were on their way to Folkestone and the *Oddfellows' Arms*—and Mr. Harry Adkins. They forced their horses into a lather, for their orders were explicit and came from one they feared.

They were big, brawny, armed with pistols and cutlasses—and as ruffianly a pair of characters as one could meet anywhere in England, either one of them alone more than a match for The Little Ferret in fisticuffs and brute strength.

"Mr. Harry Adkins, that is the man, and you will find him there," they had been told. "Keep him out of harm's way while tonight there is to be done that which has to be done. Use force if you must, and do not be put off by the fact that he has the manners and the speech of a gentleman."

"We'll give 'im wot fer," they had said. "Do fer 'im nicely we will, do 'e give any trouble."

"It will not be necessary to be *too* violent, you understand, for if you leave the fellow for dead we'll have all Bow Street, including the magistrate, around our ears," they had been ordered then. "But keep him locked up out of harm's way, and watch over him till cock's crow. He might be quite unaware of tonight's business, but we must take no chances, and this night he must be prevented at all cost from poking his nose where it is not wanted."

*   *   *

Barker, the landlord of the *Oddfellows' Arms*, had been something of a puzzle to Adkins. The Bow Street man had found it difficult to assess how much, if at all, he was implicated in smuggling—or, what was more important, how good a friend he might prove in an emergency. He was very soon to find out.

When the two thugs swaggered into the inn a number of seats in the parlour were occupied by individuals in gentlemen's clothes. They included the thieftaker, who raised his eyebrows at the sight of two such ruffianly characters invading the eminently respectable atmosphere of an inn of the standing that the *Oddfellows' Arms* enjoyed. He noted the pistols stuck in their belts and the cutlasses dangling at their sides.

"You 'ave a Mr. 'Arry Adkins biding 'ere," they informed Barker in low tones.

From a table near the door where the three stood Barker levelled expressionless eyes directly at the thieftaker and spoke in loud and sonorous tones. "You wish to know if I have a gentleman o' the name o' Mr. Adkins?" he said. "If you'll 'ave the goodness to wait, gentlemen, I'll see if I 'ave the name in the book."

Adkins rose, sauntered across the parlour and slowly ascended the stairs as the two glared down at the book on the table and the landlord's finger tracing through names they could not read.

"Ah, yes, to be sure," said Barker, when Adkins had disappeared, "I do 'ave a gentleman o' that name, and Lord keep my mem'ry sound I do remember him. But I'm afraid 'e ain't here just at the minute."

"Well, we want 'im—quick."

"Can't 'ave 'im, sirs. Leastways not at the minute. Always takes the air at this time o' night. Never misses. Won't be all that long though. Now if you'll wait in the tap room, I'll tell you the moment Mr. Adkins returns."

"We'll wait 'ere."

"You will wait in the tap room. Otherwise I won't give you a pint on the 'ouse. This way, gents."

Leading into the tap room, Barker placed ale before them. "If I may ask, wot do yer want the gentleman for?"

"We want 'im."

"I'm the landlord 'ere, and as such I'm also the law, bein' responsible for the peace o' my establishment, see? Come to that, I don't know as I should allow you in this place with those weapons you carry. I'll ask you again, gents, quite polite—wot do yer want 'im for?"

"We wants to protect 'im from 'is own folly. Keep 'im out o' 'arm's way. There's some danger down the coast. Don't want 'im to get 'urt. Friends o' 'is we are, as you might say."

"Ah," said Barker, winking. "I see. Now drink up, lads, and I'll let you know the minute 'e turns up."

Adkins, waiting in his room, opened the door to a gentle tapping—and to admit Barker, his eyes sparkling with excitement.

"Those two," he gulped. "They're arter you, sir."

"Thank you for your help, Barker," said Adkins, smiling. " 'Tis much appreciated. I think I have guessed what they're about, having added two to two and made four of it. Tonight, I'll wager, there is a run on down the coast, and they wish to keep me prisoner while it takes place. Do I guess rightly?"

"Can't be sure, but it might look like it."

"Now I will confide in you, Barker, for I take you to be a good man, and I may need your help further. I am not in these parts merely for a diversion. I am a Bow Street Runner."

Barker was smiling. "I'd guessed you was more than wot you made out, sir, and that something most decent. Quick, sir, tell me your bidding."

"First, give those two dolts some ale, with a large measure o' brandy in each pot. I'll pay for it. Meantime, I shall descend the back stairs and leave by the door to the stables.

"Second, I rather expect that Captain Richard Elias, also from Bow Street, will be back here and asking for me. Tell him, very privately you understand, that he will find me at the stable of Mr. Fordingham's house and direct him there at once."

"*Captain* Elias. Captain, eh? As good as done, sir," said Barker, winking and raising a thumb. "And Mr. Adkins, good luck, sir!"

As the landlord closed the door the thieftaker leisurely donned his cloak and top-hat, drew on his gloves, studied himself in the mirror, then picked up his cane and descended the stairs."

He was calmly waiting for a groom to saddle a horse when there was a grinding and rattling, and there was Elias pulling in his horses and leaping to the ground.

The captain drew the thieftaker out of earshot of the groom, and quickly explained what had happened in *The Floating Light*.

"Damme if you are not a born thieftaker already," said Adkins. "Excellent work, my friend. I'd guessed there might be a run tonight. Now we know for sure. And that fiddler, he might be worth interrogating sometime. Now listen carefully. There are two droll fellows in there, and they've come to take me. Imagine it, two thieves come to take a thieftaker. We could be off and leave them kicking their heels, but it would be better if they were not allowed to report on me. Get your pistol and hide near the front door."

The Little Ferret then sauntered through the front door of the inn. Topper in one hand, ebony cane tucked under an arm, he advanced towards the desk and a wide-eyed speechless Barker.

"Do not take on, my friend, for I have not taken leave of my senses," he said. "Where are they?"

The landlord drew him towards the open door of the tap room and pointed.

Adkins confronted the two ruffians with a most amiable grin. "I am told you would like to have speech with me," he said. "My name is Adkins."

"Aye, that we do," replied one, winking malevolently at his companion.

"Speak then."

"We're—we wants yer to come along o' us."

"You do, eh?" drawled the thieftaker. "Really, my fine fellows, I should be most obliged if you would start at the beginning."

"Eh?"

"Tell me where you want to take me, for instance, and why?" Adkins placed the point of his cane on the floor and lightly leant on it, one foot set firmly, the other crossed over it with toe to ground. "Do not, pray, consider me rude, but you are putting the cart before the horse, so to speak."

"We wants ter show yer summat interestin' like."

"Name it," snapped the detective.

"We dursn't." The two thugs showed signs of some discomfort.

"Why not, pray, if the matter is of interest to me?"

One of the men fingered the butt of his pistol, easing the weapon in his belt. "Now you look 'ere, sir, do as we say and no 'urt will come to you."

"What an intriguing pair of rascals you are. Damme if you don't make me most curious. Half a mind to come with you,

even if it's only for your audacity. But you're deuced imperti-
nent, for I have never set eyes on you before."

"We knows *you*."

"Ah, well maybe that makes the matter a trifle more polite.
Who am I then?"

One of the men took a step nearer and lowered his voice to
a confidential whisper. "You be a gent from Bow Street, one o'
them Runner men."

"Oh? Who said?"

"Never mind 'oo said. And listen, we'm to show you summat
that'll make yer 'air stand on end."

"Then I shall come with you."

"Right. Out the back door. Quick."

"I am so sorry to disappoint you," drawled Adkins. "But
we shall leave by the *front* door. I never go by the back door.
'Tis much too undignified."

"The back door," said one of the men, grabbing his pistol
from his belt.

"The *front* door," snapped Adkins, and with the rapidity
of a fencing master the tip of his cane was thrust painfully
in the man's chest, pushing him off balance and sending him
staggering against a table.

"All right," grumbled the man. "The front door then."

Adkins led through the parlour and preceded the two into
the night air. At once the two men drew their pistols and
levelled them at their prisoner. "Now—keep on walking, Mr.
Clever Devil," said one, "and do everything we say nice and
quiet."

Adkins walked forward, the two falling in behind him and
several feet apart. But at that moment one of them felt something hàrd jabbed into his back, and a voice roared in his
ear. "Drop your pistol this minute," were the words. "I've
got one at your back, and my finger itches to put a ball in
you."

As the man's weapon clattered down, Adkins had spun
round and with a speed of which he would have seemed in-

capable brought his cane cracking down on the other man's wrist.

For a moment Adkins's man clasped the numbed hand that had held the weapon. Then he turned to run. "Stop—or you're a dead man." The words were delivered in such a commanding tone that the man wheeled round again—to goggle at a length of slim, tapering steel glinting unwaveringly inches from his breast. And there stood Adkins, his face expressionless in the moonlight, the ebony casing of his stick in one hand and the cruel weapon it had concealed in the other.

The two policemen prodded their captives along the road until they were beyond the glow of the lamp over the inn door.

"Hand me your pistol," said Adkins to his colleague. "I don't like the things, for they may pop off at any minute, but if it be pointing at one of these rogues I'd not fret much. Now bring the curricle here with all speed."

Elias hurried off, leaving Adkins facing the two ruffians, a pistol in one hand and his unsheathed swordstick in the other. When Elias came up with the carriage he took rope from the boot, bound the prisoners at their hands and feet and wedged them into the boot, the lid of which had to remain open.

Then they drove to Fordingham's place, where they deposited the prisoners in the stable room that had been placed at Adkins's disposal.

"Call at the house," said Adkins to Elias. "My compliments to Mr. Fordingham, and tell him we shall be leaving two prisoners in this room. If he can spare a man to keep an eye on them so much the better."

As the captain left the thieftaker opened a valise he had formerly deposited in the room, took out of it a quantity of old clothes and a small wooden case. These garments he donned in the place of his elegant ones, and they included a seaman's navy-blue jersey, a dirty neckerchief, a pair of coarse, crumpled trousers and an incredibly dirty smock.

From the wooden case he took articles that had once belonged to a theatre dressing room, and began to make up his face in such a way that he would be unrecognizable to any who knew him.

When Elias returned he found the thieftaker with a strange, bulbous nose, something that resembled a swollen bruise at one side of the jaw, an untidy wig with hair falling about his ears— and the whole topped by a filthy wool cap of such antiquity that it was of indeterminable colour.

But for the detective's voice and laugh, the patrol captain would have been quite startled at his colleague's appearance.

"Drag some clothes off those louts," said Adkins, "and exchange them for your own. I apologize in advance if they infect you with some disease. Then, if you will bear with me, I shall quite alter your face with certain interesting items from this little box."

"Didn't bargain for damaging my good looks," grumbled Elias, who had regular, pleasing features and was proud of them."

"Fear not, Richard, me boy-o," smiled Adkins. "My artistic efforts will do no harm. It may be a little painful disposing of them afterwards, but you'll be as handsome a fellow as ever you were."

"Perhaps, sir," said Elias, "you will tell me what we are about?"

The results of the thieftaker's efforts on his own face produced an evil grin in the glow of the candles he had lit. "We are going to take part in a little smuggling," he said, his eyes gleaming above a distorted smile. "There is a run tonight, and in the name of good King George we're going to join it."

CHAPTER NINETEEN

THE TWO MEN from Bow Street tethered their horses in a copse a half mile beyond Dymchurch and lay in waiting under a hedge by the roadside. It was typical of the methodical, thorough Adkins that they had taken up their position with time and enough to spare before, as folk said, "the gentlemen would go by."

The night wore on, dark and silent, and when the wind gusted and the trees grumbled they shivered and moved uncomfortably from one cramped position to another. Like those for whom they waited, they prayed that the moon would not show her pale face to the world. . . .

On the wind came a sound that was not its own whispering but a distant jumble of echoes that at last became distinguishable as the clopping of horses, the trundling of wheels and the scuff of many feet.

The free traders were making a noisy march of it, arrogant and cock-sure in their knowledge that no peace-loving soul would raise a finger to interfere with their bold and unlawful operation—only maybe the revenue men—and they would seal their lips when they reached the bay. The nearest official, Ransome Quested, was a good mile away, and that grave-faced shop-keeper would be abed by now, for there were never enough riding officers to keep constant watch.

They were making a night of it, as though they went in the spring or autumn sunlight to an innocent country fair. They came with laughter on their lips and snatches of bawdy song that trailed off into shouted ribaldries and obscenities.

The horses plodded so that the men on foot could keep up

with them, and those who would play "guard" to their fellows shouldered enough weapons to equip a company of foot. The raggle-taggle cavalcade began to pass by, and the two men in hiding shivered again, but this time it was not the chill. To them, city men set down in the unfamiliar countryside, it was a weird procession indeed. The clangour and the echoes in the night made the smugglers seem like a ghost army of the dead returning to hell from a strange night out in limbo.

When the last man had passed, Adkins and Elias rose in the dark, waited for a minute and began to follow along the road. After a time they put on greater speed and gradually came up behind the rearguard.

A man looked over his shoulder. "Don't lag behind, mates," he observed. "You'll get yerselves catched by the bloody customs men—any wot 'ave the nerve, ha! ha!"

"Wot, the bloody customs men, don't make I larf," returned Adkins. "I'd eat the bastards and then spew 'em out."

"That's the spirit, mate."

"Aye, that's the spirit, mate."

They marched and marched, and the leisurely Adkins considered it was a long time since he had walked so far. The big, muscular Elias, who was used to pounding the streets of London at night-time, fared better. But Adkins cursed silently at the circumstances in which he now found himself. "God rot the damned smugglers," he said to himself vehemently. "But do 'em a mischief I will in God's good time."

They trudged on. Imperceptibly the night clouds passed on. Still there was no moon, but the sky scattered her miniature jewels to wink mysteriously at the earth, and Adkins made out the silhouette of the windmill on rising ground to his right. They must be close to the cove now.

The smugglers massed on the cliff-top, looking down. It seemed a moment when, no matter how often they came, they were struck to silence by what they saw. They discerned below them a shadow of a ship. She rode at anchor in the bay, a gently rocking shape just darker than the luminous waters, for since she gave her signal she had shown no light.

Someone seemed to be in command on the cliff-top, for he was rasping out orders. The voice struck a chord in Adkins's mind, but if he had met the fellow before he had never heard him shouting, and he was too far away to make him out by the shape of his figure.

"Jump to it, you bastard sons o' whores," yelled the voice. "Cart drivers stay here with their guard. Now you others, get down there and get the stuff moving. Rest o' the guard go with them."

Men were filing down to the beach, the foremost carrying a lantern which he raised and lowered and moved from side to side as though tracing a cross. There was a single answering blink from the ship. Then darkness.

"Stay beside the carts if you can," Adkins whispered to Elias. "Keep with the stuff they bring up and see where they take it. I shall go down to the beach. I want to keep an eye on that ship's captain when he comes off. A guinea to a hayseed it's Bart Barley."

As Adkins joined the men descending to the wet strand he heard the creak of oars as the ship's boats came with their first load. On the beach he contrived to join the circle of men who would guard the workers from attack if any came.

For this purpose he produced a pistol with which Elias had provided him from the boot of the curricle. If he remained with the guard he would have more chance of seeing Barley appear. Besides, humping heavy casks did not appeal to him overmuch.

As the first boat ground on to the shingle, the man who had appeared to be in charge on the cliff-top came forward to give more orders. He stood only a few feet from Adkins.

He was Hackett of *The Ship*.

Well, that explained something at least—why the thief-taker had been knocked on the head after telling this sly land-lord that he intended to visit the windmill. But he had pretended to Hackett to be nothing more than a curious holiday-maker. Was it also Hackett who had sent those two ruffians to the *Oddfellows' Arms* to keep watch on him while the run took place? And if so, who had told Hackett that he was a Bow Street Runner?

They were questions that would have to wait. But if this night brought nothing more, it had placed another on his list for serious interview.

Hackett was no master-mind, but he may lead him to the real chief of the smugglers.

When the boats were returning from the ship with their second load Adkins saw that one contained a man who sat in the stern and did not row. As it neared the shore the thieftaker made out the figure of Barley.

The detective moved to the end of the guard line, and in the darkness edged farther still under the lee of the cliffs.

The moment Barley leapt out of the boat it became obvious that he was superior to Hackett in the organization, for the latter became subservient in his manner to the newcomer.

Soon Barley began to stride towards the path that led to the cliff-top. Adkins followed at a distance, making as little sound as possible.

Would there be men near the top of the path? Would he be asked why he left the beach? Slowly he shadowed Barley, and was fortunate enough to slip past a number of men arguing on the manner in which one of the carts should be loaded.

Just as he had thought, Barley began to make for the wind-mill, Adkins following carefully.

Before he reached the old building, Barley unbuttoned his jacket and shirt, and took out a letter, as though to make sure he had it, returned it to its hiding place and strode on.

There was now no doubt that Barley was in fact the post-man from France, if nothing else. Was this, then, why the midshipman had met his death? Had he challenged Barley—and no doubt some other individual at the windmill—about a letter that came to England with smuggled goods?

Well, Adkins must not meet the same fate as the young naval officer, or the mystery would never be unravelled. There was sparse protection on this windy hill, only three windblown bushes, and they were some distance from the windmill. But Adkins had to hide there, for he was after bigger fish than Barley, who was no master-mind either. He whom the thief-taker wanted was the man to whom he was about to deliver the letter.

After a brief interval the detective, hiding behind the bushes, saw Barley come out of the windmill with another—a man who dwarfed the sailor, so tall and broad was he. Adkins peered from behind the bushes, but Barley's man wore a long heavy overcoat with its huge collar about his ears. The lower part of the face was muffled by a scarf, the upper portion by a mask, and a flop-brimmed hat came down over his ears. God have mercy, for the only thing he could decide from this distance was that he who had waited in the windmill was pre-cisely the size of the Vicar of Dymchurch, who was rather a giant among men. But God in heaven, for poor Susannah's sake, there were others surely with the physique of Honey-combe. . . .

The thieftaker strained his ears. He could make out only the merest scraps of conversation, but two things struck the listener as odd. The first was that the big man was talking in a sonorous monotone, as though disguising his real voice. The second was that Adkins realized he was of that relatively small number of people who could not sound the letter "r" clearly. One of those who tended to swallow the consonant instead of giving it its correct clarity. Apart from noting that the speech was educated, it was the only clue he could pick up.

So far the night had brought no real success. . . .

This mysterious gentleman could well be the brains behind the smugglers of Dymchurch. *And the murderer*. And the French spy.

But whatever part he played in the mystery, he did not con-

sort with Barley more than was necessary. Untethering a horse
from a rickety railing near the windmill, he swung himself
into the saddle, and with a peremptory goodbye to the sea
captain he was off across the downs in the direction of Dymchurch.

Barley stood for a moment as though crestfallen at the treat-
ment he had received, then began to stride back towards the
cliff-top where the loading of carts and packhorses was taking
place.

But the master of the *Kentish Maid* was no more dispirited
than the man who from behind the screen of bushes watched
him go.

The man from Bow Street clenched his fist and struck
viciously at the hard main branch of the bush, scraping skin
from his knuckles. He had seen he who must be the man he
sought most, and this mysterious gentleman, a mere shadow
in the gloom, had slipped from his grasp and vanished like a
ghostly horseman into some dark dimension known only to the
spirits of the night.

*   *   *

The brawny Elias did a night's work helping to load tubs
and cases on to the carts, and he touched his cap respectfully
when he was paid his eight shillings for his pains.

He did not see Adkins again that night, for the thieftaker
had followed Barley to the cliff-top, where the latter ordered
a horse to be found for him, mounted it and rode off. After
that the Bow Street investigator had descended to the deserted
beach and taken another look at the cave which was one of
the storehouses for contraband. He found this hideaway spot,
which had already been half-filled, stacked with barrels. The
casks that were loaded on the carts, he assumed, were the
remainder of the consignment.

The free traders and their carts and horses had long gone
from the cliff-top when the thieftaker swung his arms to in-
crease circulation, blew warmth into his hands and set off

to trudge some lonely miles to the copse near Dymchurch where his horse was tethered.

Meanwhile, Elias walked beside one of the carts. Reaching Dymchurch, the first stop was in the dark and deserted street outside *The Ship*, where some of the contraband was carried in.

Here the patrol captain took great interest in the proceedings. The normal door to the cellar was not opened. Instead the fireplace was made by some process to swing to one side, disclosing a flight of steps which led to a second cellar. In this a large amount of the tubs were deposited.

The remainder were trundled on down the high street. The horses and carts awakened the echoes in the night, yet not a shutter was moved nor a door opened.

Suddenly the procession, much smaller now, but still including Elias, halted at the double iron gates to the church—at Parson Honeycombe's churchyard. And the gates lay open—ready.

Here in the silent graveyard, among the weed-grown paths and moss-covered, tilting headstones, Captain Richard Elias, that God-fearing man of peace and humility, was to witness a strange burial.

The scene took on the atmosphere of a secret witches' Sabbath. It was the magical hour betwixt night and dawn, and from the damp earth rose a mist like devil's smoke.

The smugglers went at once to two graves. Here they lit lanterns and rested them on the earth, and the mist-dimmed glow was like the marsh lights, those luminous phenomena of the night which presaged untimely death. With iron bars they prised at the long stones that lay horizontal to the headstones. Flexing their muscles, they heaved them away to reveal nothing but empty trenches.

Not a word was spoken. There was only the scuffling of feet in the stillness, and a puffing and blowing that ejected from open mouths vapour like demon's breath.

With no word, as though even they felt some queer sense of

damaging hallowed ground, the smugglers lowered casks and wooden boxes into the false graves and laboured to replace the heavy stones in their old horizontal position.

"God's wrath on you for this." Elias wanted to bellow out the words, but he checked himself and clenched his fists. If he had done so, it was possible that the smugglers would have fled from the eerie scene, from the mist and the glow and the leaning ghosts of tombstones.

But they finished their task and dispersed, leaving Vicar Honeycombe's churchyard to its sleep.

CHAPTER TWENTY

IN THE STABLEROOM at Fordingham's place, Harry Adkins sat on the bed staring at the morning light behind the high, barred window. "Honeycombe's graveyard, eh?" he repeated, tonelessly. "Honeycombe's."

Elias, perched on a table, nodded. "That's what I said, sir."

"And Hackett's cellar, eh? Well, that does not surprise me. Nor does the churchyard if I will think aright. I am much afraid, Richard, my friend, that both the innkeeper and the parson are up to their dirty necks in this business."

"I'd say so myself."

"Logic, isn't it?" said the thieftaker. "Only logic."

"Aye, sir."

"And even if it were not for the murders and the trafficking with old Boney's men it would still have to be stopped. Did you know, Richard, that the free traders buy their tubs for thirteen shillings apiece on the Continent and if they land them duty free they can get rid of them quite easily for six times that amount?"

"I did not know it."

"Well, 'tis true. I have been reading up on the whole business of free trading. One must know everything there is to know when one is working on a case. Tobacco the smugglers get for £100 they can sell for £1,000. Some years ago one gang alone deprived the government of some £90,000 before it was broken up."

"S'truth."

"Moonrakers, huh! D'you know how the smugglers got that name? A gang of cut-throats was found at night scraping with pitchforks in their village pond, where they had hidden their contraband. They pointed to the face of the moon reflected in the water and, pretending to be simple, said they were raking for the moon. Moonrakers, eh? Soon we will have grave-rakers to contend with."

Adkins rose from the bed. "Come," he said. "We must get to work."

They washed at the pump in the yard and dressed in their normal clothes. Their two prisoners, slumped in a corner of the room, lay asleep, still bound hand and foot. Each was awakened with a bucket of water flung in the face.

"Now, my fine fellows," began Adkins. "I am indeed what you say I am, a Bow Street Runner, and I now speak to you in the name of the King and the law. Answer my questions in truth, or it will go the worse for you."

"Didn't mean no 'arm, sir," said one. "We wus only workin' under orders."

"Whose orders?"

"Don't know as——"

"Whose orders?"

" 'E'll 'ave me throat slit."

"You will have less chance of that if you help me," said the thieftaker. "I shall soon have the leaders of your gang behind bars. At the moment, all you have to answer for is an attempt to commit bodily harm. I will ask you again, who gave you orders to get me?"

The men lay morose and silent.

"Well, _I_ shall tell you who it was. Hackett."

" 'Ow did you know?"

"Never mind. Now tell me, who is the leader of the gang?"

"We only takes orders."

"All right. You take your orders from Hackett. Correct?"

"Yus."

"Who does _he_ take orders from?"

"Cap'n Barley."

"And who gives _him_ his marching orders?"

"Don't know. 'E don't know. Nobody don't know."

"Have you ever sailed with Captain Barley?"

"No, sir, we ain't seamen."

Adkins turned to Elias. "I think these men are telling the truth. Also I think they are not of much use to me, for I think I know more than they do of the matter. Have Fordingham keep them locked up here and have him feed them. I do not wish to get in conversation with Fordingham at the moment. When you have delivered my message you may drive me to Dymchurch."

In the village they went first to the churchyard, where Elias pointed out the two "graves" which now held contraband.

Adkins memorized the names on the headstones and, leaving Elias in the curricle, presented himself at the door of the vicarage.

The formalities over, he asked Honeycombe if he may borrow a quill and ink as he wished to write something down in his notebook. As he scrawled he said: "You may look over my shoulder at what I pen, sir. I think it may interest you."

This is what the vicar saw him write:

Abel Longdike, departed this life
8 Jan, 1772, in his 52nd year. Beloved
husband of Sarah.

He looked up at the parson, whose face was expressionless, then wrote:

Elijah Eccleshall, departed this life
2 Dec, 1781. God rest his soul.

Honeycombe made no comment.

"These names I have taken from headstones in your churchyard, vicar," explained the detective. "I have a good memory, but I have written them down because I do not trust it too far in matters of importance."

"Oh, and why are two graves in my churchyard of such importance, Mr. Adkins?"

"Do you not know, sir?"

"I do not."

"You surprise me, vicar. Now, sir, I will make haste to acquaint you with my true identity. I am from Bow Street in London. I am here under the orders of the chief magistrate, Sir Richard Ford, and I am not here merely to take the air, though I have taken much of it since I arrived. I must apologize for not having been frank before. But one cannot, you will appreciate, be too careful in my profession."

"You did not need to make such a long speech, sir, for I had guessed some time ago who you might be."

"Might I ask what had assisted you to this conclusion?"

"I am aware that a murder has been committed, sir, and I am, I hope, an intelligent man."

"I am sure your intellect is of the highest, vicar. And now, if you will excuse me, I must take my leave, for I have much to do."

Honeycombe showed him to the door, where he turned after descending the step on to the path. "Pardon me, sir," he said, watching the vicar's face, "but I had almost forgotten to tell you why I wanted to write down those two names. I am of a mind to obtain an order to have the graves opened up and the bodies exhumed. Good day, Mr. Honeycombe."

*   *   *

When Adkins had climbed into the curricle Elias voiced his surprise at the shortness of the visit he had paid on the vicar.

"My dear Richard," explained the detective. "It was not an interrogation—yet. I have cast a straw into the wind. I have said I will have the graves opened, but I shall tell no other. I should just like to see if the tubs vanish like magic from the churchyard. And now we will drive to the apothecary's, for I must enlist his aid in the matter."

They reached the door of the shop to meet Susannah Honeycombe leaving.

"Why, Miss Honeycombe." Adkins had leapt down from the carriage and was sweeping his hat and bowing. "It is a pleasure to see you on a morning such as this."

"Mr. Adkins." She acknowledged him briefly and turned to go.

"Miss Honeycombe. A moment if you please. Pray give me a minute of your time on so bright a day."

The lady hesitated.

"I see we have a mutual friend. I, too, was about to visit Mr. Quested."

"You are quite wrong, sir," she said, and her voice held less warmth than the early sunlight. "I have not been visiting Mr. Quested, for he is not in."

"Then there is no point in my entering his shop. Had you expected to find him this morning?"

"I had." Her eyes fell. "He had made an appointment with me, but I am told he has been called away on urgent business."

By some intuition Adkins was conscious of this moment as one of great importance, not concerning his duties so much as his personal self.

"Miss Honeycombe, I beg of you do not hurry off. I should like to have a talk with you, and I do sincerely believe it to be important." His voice was soft, gentle like falling blossom, and had it not been so the moment would have been lost for ever.

She stood very still. Slowly she raised her eyes. "If it is—important."

"I—promise you," he said.

For a moment he was short of words, and Elias, perched high on the curricle, was treated to a glimpse of his colleague that he had never been privileged to see before. This was an Adkins shorn of the supercilious voice of polite society—and momentarily of his confidence.

"I should not like to speak—of what I wish to—in the street. With good Mr. Elias here as a chaperon, will you join me in the curricle for—as long as it takes to ask you a few questions?"

"Ma'am."

Susannah looked up to see where the voice came from, and Mr. Adkins's driver, his hat doffed, had such a genial, round face and so honest a pair of blue eyes that she found herself answering his smile.

"Very well," she said, "but I cannot remain with you for long."

Adkins helped her up to the seat, and Elias, sensing the delicacy of the situation, drove slowly along the high street and even in the lane beyond kept the horses to a gentle trot.

"Miss Honeycombe," Adkins said at last. "I should like to say that I am indeed the very fellow you say I am—a peace officer from Bow Street. I had hoped you did not think I had deceived you by not admitting it to you at first."

"It is your own business, Mr. Adkins."

"Yes, it is. But I should like to say that it is a rather strange business for those who are not familiar with it."

"You speak as if I were angry with you, Mr. Adkins, and I am certainly not. I suppose we must have men to poke their noses into crime."

"I suppose we must. But I wondered. . . ."

"What did you wonder, Mr. Adkins?"

"I wondered if you were just a little annoyed that I did not take your advice and go away. I was grateful for your concern for my safety, but I should like you to understand that it was—my duty to stay."

She was smiling now and he could watch that smile for ever, but there was this duty of which he had spoken, and there were some questions he must ask. When he spoke again he knew that her smile would be gone.

"Miss Honeycombe, I am most curious to discover who told you that I was from Bow Street."

She was silent again.

"Who told you, Miss Honeycombe. Was it by any chance—your father?"

"It was not my father."

"Forgive me, Miss Honeycombe, but I am most curious. Who told you?"

"It was—Mr. Quested."

"Ah well, that would explain it, for Mr. Quested knew I was coming before I ever set off from London. You are—er, quite a friend of Mr. Quested?"

She made no reply.

"Perhaps I should not have asked. Forgive me."

"No, no. It is quite in order. Mr. Quested is one of my father's parishioners, quite an important and certainly a respectable one, and I am doing him a service."

"Ah yes, the painting. He is a painter, is he not?"

She struggled to speak. "Yes," she said at last.

He changed the subject at once, talking quickly about Dymchurch and how quaint he found it after living in London.

"Miss Honeycombe," he said then. "I have a mind to call at Mr. Quested's house, for he is one of those working with me on the matter in hand. You will know he is a riding officer?"

"Yes, I am aware of it, but I am afraid he has a hard time of it in his task to keep law and order, for there are many free traders and very few riding officers."

"It is a difficulty I find in my own work in London, where there are an hundred criminals to a mile. Miss Honeycombe, would you care to accompany me on my visit to Mrs. Quested, who may be able to tell me where I may find her husband?"

"I would rather not," said the vicar's daughter.

"She is a worthy woman, is she not?"

"Most probably, Mr. Adkins. But she is also a strange one. She appears to shut herself up in her house like a recluse, and—er, I am not on the best of terms with her."

The detective's face was grave. "There can be few who do not like such as you," he said, spontaneously. "I mean what I say, very truly."

She gave him a grateful look, but behind her eyes lay hidden shadows, and for no reason he could name the thought leapt to his mind that as far as Susannah Honeycombe was concerned Mrs. Quested was not the only strange woman in Dymchurch.

"As you please, dear lady," he said. "Where shall we deposit you? At the vicarage? In the High Street?"

"If you do not mind, sir, not at the vicarage. The High Street would do very well."

Not far from the apothecary's shop Elias drew the curricle to a halt, and leaping down Adkins helped the lady to descend.

"I know my profession is not altogether a popular one," he told her then, his hat in his hand. "People do not like to think they are spied upon. But I should so like to see you again, not to ask questions about that which I have in hand, but just to— to talk to you. I must have relaxation, even when I am working hard, and pray do not think me forward if I say what is in my mind."

"I shall try not to, Mr. Adkins."

"Then I shall say it, and I shall say it most truly. A few minutes in your company is better than sipping wine of the finest vintage."

She made no reply, for suddenly the ground became the subject of her earnest attention, and there was nothing underfoot to do so.

"Miss Honeycombe." His voice was gentle enough to surprise even himself. "May I call upon you some time when it is convenient to you? You would do me a great service."

"You may," she said, very slowly, "if you so wish."

Without raising her eyes to him, with no parting smile, unaware of his bow and his sweeping topper, she had braced herself abruptly and was now walking off in the direction of the vicarage.

Adkins sprang to his seat on the curricle, but his elation was waning before they reached the Quested home. Why, oh why was she the daughter of a vicar—*of that vicar*? And why in the name of heaven was there something unaccountable about her—as though this beautiful lady was not quite her own woman?

CHAPTER TWENTY-ONE

M RS. Q U E S T E D received Adkins in a manner of guarded shyness. Her face was white and drawn, as it had been when he had dined at the house. The riding officer had said that his wife suffered greatly with her health, and it would appear that his statement was in no way exaggerated.

"It is your good husband I should like to see," explained the detective, "and I fear I cannot find him. I wonder if you could give me some idea when and where he may be found, for he is not at his shop."

"Then he will be patrolling the coast, Mr. Adkins."

"I had thought it possible, Mrs. Quested. But his assistants in the shop say he has been called away. I thought maybe if he had gone on a journey he would have called here first to inform you, and that you might know how soon I can talk to him."

"I do not meddle in his affairs," said Mrs. Quested. "He would not thank me for it. But what is so urgent that you should visit me on the matter?"

"We are working on a case together."

"*Case*, sir?"

"Perhaps you do not understand, my dear lady. As you must know, I am from Bow Street in London, and with the help of your husband I am seeking out a criminal."

"My husband had not told me. I did not know who you were or why you were here." Her manner was vague, her voice distant.

"In that case I am sorry to have troubled you." Adkins

began to wonder if poor Quested had the difficult task of supporting a wife whose ill-health was not entirely due to physical reasons.

"Oh, do not apologize for calling, sir," said the apothecary's wife. "I have little enough company at the best of times."

"I am sorry to hear it. As a matter of fact, I nearly brought further company for you. I nearly brought Miss Honeycombe to see you——"

"Miss Honeycombe! That hussy!" Suddenly Mrs. Quested had lost her apathy. Her eyes flamed and her voice became high-pitched. "Do not bring such as *her* here. Never! Never, I say."

"You do not like Miss Honeycombe then?"

"I do not."

"I must admit to some little surprise, Mrs. Quested. I thought her most charming."

"You would, sir. You are a man, are you not? And she is young and pretty and——" Mrs. Quested stopped abruptly.

"I should say, Mrs. Quested, respecting your observations, that she cannot help being young—or pretty."

"Well, I suppose you would like her, specially if you were one of *those*."

"One of—*what*, dear lady."

"*You* know."

"I am afraid I do not."

"Well, of course you do, sir. There is a kind of man—or gentleman, and they're the worst—who are ever watching for *that* kind of woman to have of her what they will. Besides, she's young and pretty."

"I hope you do not include me——"

"She's a hussy. Do not speak of her in my presence."

"I beg your pardon, Mrs. Quested. I shall not then." Adkins had been conscious of a sense of gloom in the presence of this woman, and the talk of Susannah had increased it tenfold. He would not prolong his departure. "Now, about your husband, Mrs. Quested, about whom I really came to see you. Do not be concerned about my questions, for I shall find him soon no doubt."

"I do not know where he is. Had it been a Wednesday I might have been able to help you, sir. It is always on a Wednesday he goes to Folkestone to see Mr. Fordingham."

"Well, it is not a Wednesday, so I shall not trouble you further. Good day, Mrs. Quested."

Adkins left the apothecary's lady wishing he had never called upon her. Rattling on their way to Folkestone, he remained silent and thoughtful, and Elias, affected by his colleague's depression, remained quiet.

The thieftaker's brow was still black when he called upon Fordingham.

"I have some information that will please you," he told the customs official. "I now know of three places where contraband is hidden away."

"Excellent!" exclaimed the excise chief. "Tell me at once where they are and we shall have the places raided."

"Not so fast, sir," said the detective. "The matter is now more serious than smuggling. In the interests of national security we are searching for one man—and he must be found soon. If you swoop on all three places it will put the free traders too much on their guard, and I think it is they who will lead me to the man I seek."

"Drat it man, I have my job to do. Tell me where all this contraband is. I have my job to do."

"And I mine. However, I propose to tell you, Mr. Fordingham, where one quantity of goods lies, for I want your help in the matter, and I hope the time may not be long delayed when I give you the word to go after the other two. I do not think now that I am working entirely in the dark, but I do not want what I have accomplished ruined. Now do I have your word that you will follow my instructions to the letter?"

"I promise."

"Very well. In the churchyard at Dymchurch there are two

graves which at this moment contain casks instead of bodies. I should like you to send men to examine those graves. But I do not want this done tonight. I should like your men to move in *tomorrow* night. You see, I have told one man— and one only, besides yourself—that the graves are to be tampered with by the authorities. We shall give him one night to get the stuff shifted——"

"And lose it? Are you mad?"

"Are *you* mad, Mr. Fordingham? I am testing the gentleman concerned. If the stuff is still there *tomorrow* night, then the man I suspect might be innocent. If it is gone, he will most certainly be guilty. Give him a night to move the stuff—if he be guilty. Do as I say, sir, and leave the operation until *tomorrow* night—or in the name of King George you will have a great deal to answer for. Do not forget that I am retained also on this case by the Secretary for War. I take it you now understand my reasoning—and the importance of the matter?"

"I do, Mr. Adkins. I shall do as you say."

The thieftaker then gave Fordingham the text of the epitaphs so that the graves could be found, and the "exhumation" was fixed for midnight on the following day.

Adkins then went to the *Oddfellows' Arms* and sat morosely in his room, having shouted for a fire to be lit in it and a bottle of wine to be brought.

He slumped into a chair, but the glow of both fire and wine did not improve a growing sense of despair. Never before had he been placed in the position where he might have to take a guilty man against all his wishes—because that man was the father of a woman he could not get out of his thoughts.

He no longer thought of this man as the Vicar of Dymchurch, or even as plain John Wyndham Honeycombe, if that were what he turned out to be. Now the fellow entered his mind only as "Susannah's father."

God rot the man, for if it were not he, who else might it be who master-minded the gang? Damn the circumstance that had put him on the assignment. Yet if he had not been sent, he would never have met Susannah. . . .

Not have met Susannah. Well, that was a laugh, too. For what had she done so far to show the slightest interest in him? She had smiled rather prettily, and he was certain that she was sad about something. But a girl could smile at a man out of nothing but politeness.

In his morbid state yet another thought came. It came with terrifying suddenness, like a blow from a man one had once called a friend. Susannah herself might be caught up in the net of crime that seemed to strangle this mysterious part of Kent. Certain it was that she, like so many others, had not wanted him there.

But the thing that worried him most at this moment was that he had now asked to meet her socially, and with the suspicions he had in his mind he had not possessed the right to do so. Maybe the sensible thing would be not to seek her out, to avoid her company, never to see her again. . . .

With a sudden, vicious movement, he flung the glass from which he was drinking into the fireplace, where it shattered to a hundred fragments and left wine like splotches of blood on the hearthstone. He rose and paced the room.

There was a time in the life of every thieftaker, they said, when he would be tested more than he had been before—or would ever be again. For Harry Adkins that time was now.

He did not at first hear the knock on the door, and the rapping had to be repeated before he paused and summoned the visitor to enter. It was Barker with a letter.

"Came from the London mail coach, Mr. Adkins. Thought you'd like to 'ave it right away."

The detective took it absent-mindedly, with a murmur of thanks. But when the landlord withdrew and closed the door he found himself staring at the handwriting of his colleague in London, John Clark, whose help he had sought in relation to Susannah's father.

He tore open the envelope and read these words:

Dear Harry,

You did ask me to look into the matter of a Gentleman of the name of John Wyndham Honeycombe. I have looked in the Books of Reference, and if you suspected the said Gentleman of masquerading as a priest when he was not, I am afraid you are wrong, for he is most certainly a Reverend Gentleman. He is indeed a Clerk in Holy Orders, being fully qualified in Theology, a Master of the Arts and having been fully ordained in the year 1779. He held curacies in Cornwall before being given the Living of the Parish of Dymchurch in the year 1792.

I am sorrie if you are disappointed, but these are the true facts, and I shall enjoy a drink at your expense in full payment of my services!

As to my parte in the Matter, I have firmly established that the murder of the two French émigrés who resided in London must have been at the hand of a French wolf in sheep's clothing, but so far I have been unable to gain a lead on him. Whether he lives at my end of the Puzzle or at yours is still unknown.

But whoever he may be, he is no doubt one of Nap's spies, and an Assassinator Extraordinary. So we must find him before he does further damage.

Yours,

John Clark

Crumpling the letter in his hand, Adkins held it for a moment, breathing heavily, before throwing it into the fire. His eyes gleamed as, standing very still, he watched the paper curl as the flames caught it.

So, unlikely as it had seemed, Susannah's father really was the Reverend John Wyndham Honeycombe. Once he had wanted confirmation that this was not so. Now he was far from disappointed.

Could this give him an excuse—for it could be no more than an excuse—for renewing his acquaintance with Susannah?

The next moment he was rapping on the door of Captain Elias's bedroom and entering with a firm step. "We rise early tomorrow," he said, "for we are off to Dymchurch. There is a whole day to await events, and I intend to spend at least part of it with the delectable Miss Honeycombe."

But when he went to bed it was a long time before sleep came. For what did Clark's letter prove? That the distinctly Reverend John Honeycombe was only very slightly less under suspicion than he had been before.

CHAPTER TWENTY-TWO

THE CURRICLE DREW up outside the vicarage, and Adkins was thudding at the big iron knocker, and a man-servant, who appeared too large and muscular for his job, was surveying the visitor coldly.

"I should like to see Miss Honeycombe—and, er, Mr. Honeycombe, too. My name is Adkins."

"Please to wait," growled the servant, leaving Adkins on the step and the door half-closed.

He returned in a few moments to say: "Sorry, sir, but vicar says he be too busy to see you."

"Then return to Mr. Honeycombe, if you please, and inform him that I am much too busy *not* to see him."

The servant hesitated, for he was paid a great deal more by the parson than the three shillings a week he had earned as a farm labourer, and he did not wish to lose his job.

"Do my bidding," said Adkins, and there was a hard edge to his voice.

The servant did his bidding, returning to say: "Vicar will see you, sir, but only for a moment. Enter if you please."

The visitor was shown to the drawing room, a long apartment luxuriously furnished. Adkins was a man who knew good things when he saw them, and could hazard a guess at the price of them. With the eye of a connoisseur, he noted that the antimacassars on chairs and couches were of the finest lace, the furnishings of the best. Rich satin covered the chaise-longue. The silver would have been more in keeping with the main rooms of a bishop's palace than a country vicarage, and the visitor reckoned that some of the ornaments were priceless.

Perhaps he should write another letter to John Clark to discover just what the living of Dymchurch amounted to in pounds per year.

Honeycombe greeted him with a forced smile. "What is it you want, sir, for I am a busy man?"

"I do not doubt it, parson, and I apologize for disturbing you."

"Well, what is it, man? Have you come to ask questions, for that appears to be your stock in trade?"

"Strange as it may appear, sir, on this occasion I have not. 'Tis a social visit, nothing more. Your daughter has been pleased to say that she will accept a social visit from me."

"Oh?" The parson was scowling.

"Indeed she has, sir. Consequently, I am here to ask your permission to walk and talk with her. It is a day to be out of doors, do you not think?"

"Why should I give you such permission?"

"Because I am led to believe that she wishes it—as I do myself. I find her company of the most charming."

"Why should I allow my daughter to—er, consort with a man from Bow Street?"

"Why should you *not* allow her to consort with a *gentleman* from Bow Street?"

"Because I do not wish you to ask her questions. Er, I do not wish her to be troubled."

"I do not propose to ask her questions. I propose merely, with your permission, to take the air with her."

"You do, eh?"

"I do."

"Well, I should want your word as—a gentleman—that you will not worry her with questions and that you will be honourable with her as—a gentleman."

"Agreed on both counts, sir. You have my word—as a gentleman."

"Then we shall see if it is her wish——"

The door opened and in walked Susannah. "I knew you were here, Mr. Adkins," she said. "I saw your curricle."

"Am I to understand you wish to meet Mr. Adkins socially, my dear?" asked the vicar.

"I do, father. I gave him permission to call upon me."

"Very well, then. God be with you." Parson Honeycombe left the room with the deepest of frowns upon his forehead.

*   *   *

They walked the bosky path among the trees for which Dymchurch had two names—Darkness Dell and Lovers' Wood, one for winter and the other for summer, the locals having a quaint idea that there was a special season for falling in love.

That there was a time of year for making love out of doors was indisputable, but there was a saying that poor man's wooing had to be done before the "last bee and wassup died."

Watching them take the path into the wood, Elias grinned. Waiting for them with the curricle, he chuckled from time to time, remembering that there were good-natured tales told of the celebrated Harry Adkins and his way with the wenches, recalling having once overheard Sir Richard Ford declare that he did not care how many maids Adkins bedded so long as he continued to bring in the thieves and murderers.

The captain had no doubt in his mind what his dapper colleague was about in the dappled silence of the wood.

They were lost from his view now, for the path was like a gigantic, mottled snake that had died a thousand years ago as it threaded sunshine and shadow searching for an Eve with an apple and an Adam naked in the trees.

For a time as they walked they fell silent under the spell of Lovers' Wood, for the snow had long melted from its roof of branches, and it would not be Darkness Dell again until Autumn married November's mists.

Susannah was the first to speak. Her eyes had lost that strange shadow of sadness, her voice its strained tone. She told him some of the quaint, fanciful names the rustics used for the wild flowers and the insects they passed on their way. The sophisticated man from the city watched and listened. This was no scheming woman, no hussy, as the sour-faced Mrs. Quested had dubbed her. Instead she was a woman with charm and simplicity rooted in her childhood.

"Look, a devil's coach horse," she exclaimed—and it was a caterpillar. A bumble bee was to her a "hummer bee," the foxgloves in her language became "fairies petticoats," the the pimpernel "poor man's weatherglass" or "wink-a-peep." And the meadow-sweet became on the instant "maid of the mead."

He did not understand half of what she said, save that it showed a goodness in her that life had not spoilt. She babbled on like a stream in spate, and he quite content to float his mind like a twirling leaf on the rushing waters of her words.

He stooped to pick for her a handful of her beloved wild flowers, and she knelt quickly beside him and put her hand on his to prevent it.

"No," she said vehemently. "No, Mr. Adkins. Let them be. Pluck them and they will die."

"You—do not want them to die?" His voice was as gentle as the pressure of her hand on his.

"I do not want anything to die," she whispered. "I believe that the things that grow have a life like ours, and that God makes them die when it is time for them to die. The trees have a long life, so much longer than ours, but the flowers have so short a time, and they are so lovely."

"What a lovely person you are—Susannah." He paused, and she did not object to his use of her given name, or did not say so.

"Susannah." He tried it again, very softly, lest she had not heard.

But she had heard the first time—and the second—and she would listen to him repeating her name as often as he cared. She was looking at him, her glance unwavering. His own passed slowly to her mouth, which was very close to his. His movement was almost imperceptible as his lips brushed hers as lightly as a resting butterfly.

"Susannah." There was nothing else he could think of saying, or wanted to say.

He took both her hands in his and slowly they rose until they stood upright. But the low-hung branches of the trees shaded the sunlight, and suddenly the shadow of sadness was in her eyes again.

His hands crept round her waist, but she stepped back. "No," she said.

"Why not?" he asked.

"I cannot," she said. "Do not ask me why."

They walked on, but he did not release one of her hands. They moved in shadow and in sunlight. The murmurings of the wood grew louder. The sun rose higher. The day grew warmer.

"Forgive me, Susannah, for I have no right to ask," he said at last, "but something tells me that there was a time when you were happier than you are now."

She sighed, or it was the breeze, and he did not think she would ever answer.

"You are most—perceptive," she said then. "You are also—quite right."

"Tell me to seal my lips if you wish it," he said, but she remained silent and he went on speaking. "You were happy when you were a child. Is it so?"

"Yes."

"And something has happened to make you less happy?"

"You know me but little, yet you see me very well," she said, and it was an answer in the affirmative, "or you are a very good thieftaker for finding what you seek."

"I am not a thieftaker today," he said, very gravely. "I am Harry Adkins—no more. I am taking a day off duty, and I have sworn not to ask any questions at all. I shall ask you but one more—may I see you again?"

"You may."

He found himself squeezing her hand, and her returning the pressure. "You said just now that I see you very well. I think I do, and I like what I see."

"Thank you," she said.

"And if I am as perceptive as you suggest," he persisted, "I think perhaps we know—each other—very well."

"I think perhaps," she said, "we do."

When they reappeared from the wood, still hand in hand, Elias stifled a smile. He may be forgiven for thinking what he did, but he would have been astounded to discover that Adkins had not even kissed her—well, not properly anyhow.

* * *

Susannah Honeycombe came back to the vicarage with a glow in her face that her father had not seen for a long time. A new radiance from within was lighting her eyes.

"You would appear to have had a pleasant time with—our man from Bow Street?" he asked.

"I have, father," she replied. "He is a most likeable person."

"Ah well, perhaps so, when he is not exerting his authority." The vicar was watching his daughter closely. "At any rate, he would not appear to have worried you."

"Of course not, father. He was most agreeable."

"He did not pester you with questions, then?"

"No."

"Then he kept his promise to me, and I am glad of it. What are your plans for the afternoon, Susannah?"

"I am to see Mr. Quested," she said.

The words ended the conversation. She walked slowly out into the garden. She had quite forgotten until then her appointment with the local portrait painter, and she would not have been reminded of it so soon after saying her farewells to the man from London.

The birds went chirpily about their summer business, and she did not hear them. The sun shone on the garden flowers, and they no longer possessed romantic names. In her new mood the garden rushes possessed their Latin name instead of being "red hot pokers" and the border of London Pride was not composed of "queen's feathers" any more.

For she had an appointment with Mr. Quested, and there were things which happened in that room above his shop that did not bear thinking of.

CHAPTER TWENTY-THREE

THE LANTERNS IN the graveyard glowed like wills-o'-the-wisp over the Romney marshes. The midnight silence was intense, the tread of feet eerie and the shadows of the revenue men like ghosts rising from the mist.

Mr. Customer Fordingham himself was there to superintend so exciting a prospect of discovering hidden contraband. With him to see for themselves if anything—or nothing—were uncovered were the two men from Bow Street.

Now the three stood together behind the headstone which proclaimed faintly in the light of an upraised lantern the resting place of the long-dead Abel Longdike. They had travelled together from Folkestone in Fordingham's own coach, followed by a dozen men riding horses, dressed in white, bell-bottomed trousers, dark jackets and black hats and carrying digging implements as well as arms.

The silent churchyard was filled with shadows, and the men, tight-lipped and grim-faced, could have sworn that some of them moved. The exercise did not appeal to a single man, for tampering with graves was to them like the work of witches and warlocks on a night when ther secret coven was at its devilish work. Even Fordingham, Adkins and Elias, shifting their feet and coughing nervously, were strangely silent.

The grating of crowbars and the clink of metal on stone echoed in the midnight hush, and Adkins looked anxiously towards the vicarage nearby. Every window was in darkness—and remained so.

The men prised at the heavy, horizontal stone that covered the grave, and at last heaved it clear.

Adkins sprang forward and gazed down. All that was to be seen was soil.

Had the stuff been taken away?

"Dig," he snapped, stepping back.

But when the men bent to their task their spades soon struck something hard. A few inches of soil were shovelled away, and Adkins and Fordingham were suddenly gazing at the tops of casks.

One after the other, barrels of brandy were heaved out. Then came boxes of tobacco.

The party moved, examining more headstones until the light of their lanterns showed the name of Elijah Eccleshall, dead these twenty years and more.

Here they set to work again, and this also was found to be full of contraband.

"Impound these goods," ordered the district customs chief. "Back to Folkestone with them. But first fill in the graves and leave all as you found it."

When this was done Fordingham, whom Adkins had once briefly suspected, did an action that commended him to the thieftaker. He moved to the first grave that had been opened and stood beside it with bowed head. Then he made over it the sign of the cross and spoke words he thought apt and necessary in the circumstances.

"Abel Longdike, departed this life, to wherever your coffin has been removed, may you rest in peace."

This impromptu little ceremony he repeated at the grave which had once held the remains of Elijah Eccleshall.

The coach jolted a great deal on the return journey to Folkestone, for after the night's work and its weird sense of the sacrilegious the driver was anxious to be home and abed. But the comfort-loving Adkins, sitting silent and thoughtful in a corner of the vehicle, was almost unaware of the bumping and rattling.

For suspicion was lifting like morning's incense from the broad shoulders of Susannah's father, and he was glad of it.

It would seem that Parson Honeycombe had known of no reason why the two graves should be opened, and had been unafraid. At first Adkins was numbed by the realization. Then his thoughts began to flow, and he dared to feel relieved, to be glad at the result of this night's work for Susannah's sake. For dear Susannah. . . .

He had been so near to making an arrest. Now it would seem he had to tackle the whole matter anew, and many a thieftaker might have been annoyed instead of glad.

"Mr. Fordingham," he said, squaring his shoulders in the dark coach, "I shall have to do some re-thinking."

"The reason being, no doubt, that he you suspected may now appear innocent. Whom did you suspect?"

"Susannah's—er, Parson Honeycombe."

"Parson Honeycombe?" The customs man was incredulous. "A man of the cloth?"

" 'Tis a long story. You must believe I had good reasons. But now I would ask of you to forget I ever suspected the fellow— and to treat the matter as extremely confidential."

"You have my promise. Do you suspect any other?"

"I suspect many of taking part in smuggling. Now I shall have to force my attention on them, and they will not be over-pleased about the matter. They will have to face questions they may find difficult to answer. But I am as far away from finding my murderer as heaven is from hell."

Fordingham fell silent for a time. "Does this mean there will be a delay in raiding the other places where you have found hidden contraband?"

"I am afraid it does."

"A pity. Tonight I have one feather in my cap. I should have liked it to be three."

"It *will* be three, if you will have patience, sir. And if the murder is brought out into the open I'll wager your coast will be largely free of smugglers for some time to come."

Fordingham eased himself into a more comfortable position as the coach rounded a bend in the road. "I do not know much about your profession, Mr. Adkins, but I take it you have tonight received a setback after a great deal of work. I marvel, sir, at your patience and optimism."

"Without either," was the reply, "I would not be much of a thieftaker."

"What will you do now, Mr. Adkins?"

"Just wait," said the detective. "Wait for inspiration."

They were driving into Folkestone when Adkins spoke again, and it was in the manner of thinking aloud. "Now there's Hackett, he'll get a grilling from me. . . . And Barley, I'll ask him so many questions he won't know what day of the week it is. . . . I'll enlist the help of Quested. . . . Haven't told him yet about the night of the run and what I discovered then. . . . I'll see Quested tomorrow, which is Tuesday, for I would be unable to find him the day after."

"Why so, Mr. Adkins?"

" 'Tis the day he visits you, Mr. Fordingham."

" 'Tis nothing of the kind."

"That is strange, Mr. Fordingham. I understood he visits you on a Wednesday and makes a day of it."

"He has never been to see me on a Wednesday. I know it to be so, for it is the day I travel to a town some distance north on business."

The thieftaker's hand was at his chin, stroking it thoughtfully. "This is remarkable, Mr. Fordingham. Why should his wife think he visits you on a Wednesday? Very remarkable. Very remarkable indeed. By the way, Mr. Fordingham, where do you go on these Wednesdays?"

"As I have said, I travel north—on business."

In his bed at the *Oddfellows' Arms* Adkins lay very much awake. Where did Ransome Quested go on a Wednesday? Tomorrow he would pay a call on him, and that would be one question in his pack that he would hold as an ace.

*   *   *

Ransome Quested was sitting in the room above his shop, staring with glazed yet fervent eyes at a painting of Susannah Honeycombe which he had propped up before him on his desk. Susannah herself would have been astounded if she had seen it, for although she had sat for the portrait stripped to the waist, he had painted in the rest of her body, quite nude, in her absence, and even an art critic might have assessed the work as obscene.

"Yes?" His reply to the tapping on the door was delivered in a vague and distant manner, as though he had not yet awakened from some exotic reverie. "Come in."

"A visitor to see you, sir," said one of his young assistants, catching a glimpse of the obscene portrait. "Mr. Adkins, sir."

"Mr. Adkins?" Suddenly Quested was on his feet. "Ah, yes, Mr. Adkins. Show him up, but wait—keep him a moment before doing so."

"Very good, sir." The young man took one more fleeting glance at the portrait, and managed to stifle a giggle until he had closed the door behind him.

The apothecary's dream-like attitude ceased abruptly. He grabbed the portrait and placed it in a corner of the room beside others and near to his easel—its face to the wall. When Adkins entered he was sitting at his desk, his finger-tips together on his breast and his eyes alert once more.

"Always pleasant to see you, Mr. Adkins," he simpered, "and to what do I owe the pleasure of this visit?"

"I come with news which as a riding officer should interest you, Mr. Quested. I have just heard that another run has taken place. It may be but a rumour. There are so many of 'em on this coast that I am quite baffled, sir. But have you heard anything yourself? Is it possible that the gossipmongers are correct?"

"Yes, Mr. Adkins, I had heard similar talk, and I am most displeased about the matter, for if it be true then I am not as efficient as I might be. God rot the brandy runners. They are too rapacious by half, the devil-rotted cut-throats. A run

under my very nose, eh? Rare it is for the contrabanders
to stage a run and Ransome Quested not to hear a whisper.
But that is the case this time, I'm very much afraid."

The riding officer paused for his visitor to speak. But it was
as though Adkins had been struck temporarily dumb. He stood
as still as a statue, his brain whirling but his face by long
practice expressionless.

*God in heaven what was this? Well spoken though he
was, Quested was demonstrating an idiosyncrasy of speech,
and by Jupiter what an interesting one! The apothecary
had just delivered a short speech containing an unusually
large number of words containing the letter "r," and apparently he was a man who found it somewhat difficult to sound
this letter clearly, tending to swallow it rather than pro-
nounce it.*

"Mr. Adkins, take a seat."

Adkins remained standing *The peculiarity was precisely the
odd thing he had noted in the speech of the man who had met
Barley at the windmill as the thieftaker had hidden in the
bushes.*

"Pray take a seat, sir."

The thieftaker stood gazing forward.

Devil take it, why had he not noted the peculiarity before?

"Mr. Adkins, does something ail you? I have asked you
twice to take a seat and you stand as though turned to stone."

"Yes, Mr. Quested, there *is* something that ails me. It is
the same emotion that besets your good self. Like you, I am
angry that the free traders should have made a run under my
nose and me as innocent of it as a babe. Did they but know,
my superiors at Bow Street would not be liking me at this
moment."

"Do not fret, Mr. Adkins, for I shall not tell them. I am
myself failing in my duty—or it would seem very much like
it."

The thieftaker was aware that he wished to do some deep

thinking, and he must get away from the fellow in order to do so.

"I must take my leave, Mr. Quested, for even at this late hour I must try to discover something about that run. You will excuse me, sir, and might I ask that if you discover any details of the run you will inform me of them at the soonest?"

"I shall, sir," said the riding officer. "I most certainly shall."

Elias drove a silent and meditative Adkins back to Folkestone.

Could the detective possibly suspect Quested? Why, it was the riding officer himself who had suggested calling for help from Bow Street. . . .

But was it so fantastic to believe the man guilty? Come to think of it, the fellow was every inch as tall and broad as Parson Honeycombe. Of course, one had expected a riding officer to be of good physique, but by all the saints the man was exactly the height and build of the man who had waited at the windmill—no doubt to receive the letter Skipper Barley carried.

The thieftaker's thoughts wandered down hitherto unexplored channels. Ransome Quested was also a man of many parts. An apothecary. A riding officer. A painter. In the lord's name, what other interests did he have?

Neither was it beyond imagination that the austere and dignified shopkeeper was a hard man. Look at the wife and often you found the husband. Could it be that Quested had dominated his poor wife into that state of nervous dejection?

The new theory was as pregnant with possibilities, Adkins told himself, as a dairy maid seven months with child. Who could be better than a riding officer, who must know a deal about free trading, to be taking an important and unknown part in it? What a splendid deception it would be to become appointed a riding officer? Whoever would then suspect the man?

And why were the authorities so seldom alerted when a run was to be made? Well, who was the man who should ride with the news as though hell's hounds were at his ankles? The riding officer, of course.

It would not be beyond the man's wit to put on a different voice whenever it might be necessary. And come to think of it, the fellow lived very well for an apothecary, even though his business ran to two assistants.

Ransome Quested, the shopkeeper who sported himself like a squire, could do with a little watching, starting from to-morrow—which was a Wednesday.

CHAPTER TWENTY-FOUR

THE LITTLE FERRET was as much an artist at theatre make-up as the puritanical apothecary at painting nudes.

It was yet dark as he sat before a mirror with his wooden box at his side, giving himself black, bushy eyebrows and a straggly dark beard and moustache. When he had finished his nose was twice its normal thickness and somewhat splayed towards his cheeks, and the wig he securely attached to his head would have done justice to that of a pantomime devil. All in all, every pleasant feature, of which his face had many, had temporarily vanished, leaving him with an altogether unwholesome appearance.

From his valise he took a swallow-tail coat of scuffed and shiny black and a yellow waistcoat which he had splashed with stains. He wore a broad-brimmed, flat hat neither as elegant nor modish as his topper, and breeches and hose instead of his immaculate riding boots.

Thus attired and mounted on a chestnut cob he presented himself to a silent and deserted world as the dawn painted pale streaks in the night sky. Harry Adkins was to make quite certain that the apothecary would not set out on his mysterious Wednesday journey before he could be at Dymchurch to watch him go.

It meant, of course, for the comfortable thieftaker a very uncomfortable wait, hidden with his horse behind a hedge opposite the entrance to the gracious Quested home.

For a long time the detective stamped about in the dew-drenched grass, blowing into his hands to warm them, and an itch in his nostrils threatening to produce a sneeze at any moment.

At last Quested appeared, mounting his horse and making off in the direction of Hythe and Folkestone. Adkins allowed him to make some distance before leading his horse through a gap in the hedge and setting off to follow him.

At an inn yard at Hythe stood the London coach, and Adkins rode in just in time to see Quested talking to the guard, leaving his horse in charge of an ostler and entering the inn.

"When are you off?" Adkins asked of the guard.

"Under the 'arf hour," was the reply.

"Glad I'm in time to join you," said Adkins, smiling.

"You ain't."

"I ain't what?"

"You ain't a-coming with us."

"Why not?"

"No room."

"Well, what about the gentleman who was just talking to you? No room for him?"

"Booked 'is seat yesterday."

"You could squeeze me in up top, eh?"

"Couldn't get you in if you was King George."

Adkins spun a golden guinea and caught it. "I think perhaps you could squeeze me in."

"It'd be very 'ard," said the guard, eyeing the coin.

"Hold out your hand," ordered Adkins, and when the guard had done so he dropped the guinea into his palm. "I'll go inside and book my ticket."

"Right you are, sir," said the guard, his long face widening perceptibly. "Tell 'em guard says there's room atop."

Adkins booked to London, thinking the money well spent even if his quarry alighted before the city was reached.

The thieftaker was already in his seat on top of the coach when Quested came from the inn. His high-collared greatcoat was similar to that worn by the man who had met Barley at the windmill.

This was the London Flyer, and it made good speed, stopping only to allow a passenger to alight at Ashford.

Later in the yard of the *Royal Star* at Maidstone Quested climbed down, and from his high perch Adkins saw him look rapidly about him as though looking for someone. Adkins descended in time to hear his quarry asking if the southbound London coach had arrived. Apparently it had not, and Quested loitered in the yard.

So did Adkins, making conversation with an ostler but keeping an eye on Quested, who strode to a wooden bench in the yard and sat down.

The apothecary swept his gaze round—and fixed it on the thieftaker. He was taking an uncomfortably long stare.

Adkins gazed back at him squarely, and Quested, who seemed a little nervous, dropped his eyes to the cobbles. There had been no sign of recognition, and the thieftaker's confidence in his disguise returned.

Eventually a posthorn echoed, and soon the coach from London rattled in. From it descended a pale-faced gentleman wearing dark, modish clothes and a dignified and sober expression.

Quested rose at once and met the newcomer half-way across the yard. To all appearances, thought Adkins, here were two of the most respectable gentlemen in existence. They were near enough for the watcher to hear the beginning of their conversation.

"Morning, Mr. Manners," said Quested.

"Morning, Mr. Adams," was the reply.

"Had a long wait," said Quested, alias Adams. "Came by coach today. Had to take an early one to be in time."

"Why by coach?" asked the man addressed as Manners, a hint of alarm in his voice. "You've come alone I hope."

"Of course I am alone. My chaise requires repairs, and it has cost me all of fifteen shillings to travel by coach."

"You have my deepest sympathy, Mr. Adams, you skinflint. Have you booked the room?"

"No."

"Didn't think you had. Obviously, you leave me to pay for it. You do not change, Mr. Adams. Well, let us get inside."

The moment they disappeared within the door, Adkins followed, but he was not in time to hear which room they had been given. He watched them mount the stairs, then presented himself to the innkeeper.

"I need your help," he rapped. " 'Tis urgent."

The normally immaculate Adkins, however, was at a disadvantage because of his disguise. For the landlord, who judged his fellows by their clothing (and was not unusual in this respect) looked down haughtily on the ill-dressed little individual, noting at once the shabby jacket and stained waistcoat.

"I do not know as how I am h'inclined to help you," he declared pompously.

"Quickly, man. The two gentlemen who have just arrived. Which room have you given them?"

"Don't care to say, that I don't."

"Listen, my good fellow. I am from Bow Street in London. I am here on the authority of the magistrate. It is a matter of crime."

There was an unmistakable authority in the voice, for all his shabbiness, and the innkeeper was becoming aware of it.

"How do I know you be such?" said the landlord, less pompously.

From his jacket pocket Adkins whipped out a set of wrist manacles, dangling them an inch from the surprised landlord's nose. "Is it every visitor carries these?" he demanded. "The room number at once, if you please, or it will go ill with you."

"Room number—five," was the hesitant reply. "Marked on the door. But I don't want no trouble."

"You won't get any," snapped Adkins. "Listen carefully. I am going to allow both these gentlemen to leave without accosting them. There will be no trouble, but do not on any account allow anyone to know I am from Bow Street."

He did not wait for a reply, but bounded up the stairs and put his eye to the large keyhole of Room No. 5. He was not in time to see Quested hand over the letter, but this must have been so, for the man called Manners was reading one.

The man from the London coach took a seat at a table and began to write what Adkins assumed to be a reply to the message he had received. This, together with money, was handed to Quested.

The thieftaker did not wait longer, but hurried downstairs and again sought out the landlord.

"Have you seen these men before?" he asked.

"They meets here reg'lar," was the reply.

"What happens after the meetings?"

"The big man—he usually drives himself in a chaise—takes the road south. That would appear also to be the direction he comes in from. The other takes the next coach back to London."

"When are the coaches due?"

"The one for the south very shortly, sir. The one for London an hour later. But listen 'ere, sir, do I get into any trouble?"

"Not if you keep your lips sealed and behave quite naturally. Now I shall merely take a seat in that somewhat dark corner there. That is all I shall do."

"Thank you, sir. I don't want no——"

"Trouble," said Adkins. "Landlord, my thanks to you."

Adkins, sitting watching the staircase, had already decided what he must do. He knew where to find Quested later. He must hang on to the man from London, allowing the apothecary to return blissfully to Dymchurch.

Soon Quested descended the stairs alone and took a seat in the southbound coach. Later the coach for London carried among its passengers both Manners and Adkins.

When he alighted in the city, the French spy was never for

a moment aware that he was followed to his lodgings, or that when the door closed behind him a figure of somewhat unkempt appearance noted the number of the house and the name of the street—and made his way with all haste to the public office in Bow Street.

CHAPTER TWENTY-FIVE

ADKINS FOUND HIS fellow thieftaker, John Clark, in the *Brown Bear* opposite the Bow Street office, quickly gave him a description of the man he had trailed from Maidstone and stated where he could be found.

"Calls himself Manners," he explained. "But deuced if he has any English blood in him. Should say it's a certainty he holds rank in the French intelligence service. Wager he's a spy all right."

"And our mass murderer."

"Aye, and that, too."

"Well, Harry, I'll bring him in and if it be necessary question him till Judgment Day."

"I'll leave that to you, John," said Adkins, "for I am off this minute back to Kent. I'll get me a fast chaise and set off with no supper, or a sandwich to eat on the way, for I have no time to lose. I must get there before a certain ship named the *Kentish Maid* sails for France. There is a letter to intercept—and some unfinished business to attend to."

"Right, and I'm off this minute to take our mysterious Mr. Manners—or Capitaine whatever his real name is. Harry, me boy-o, you've done excellent work, and made the job easy for me. I'll take a patrol captain and four men with me, and have him under lock and key before midnight. Soon put an end now to the games he plays in this country."

They hurried across Bow Street to where the lamps burned all night and set about their arrangements.

Within the quarter hour Adkins was perched on the high seat of a light chaise, a patrolman handling the reins beside him, and rattling through the night on the main road south with a full moon to light their way.

They came to Folkestone in the shy morning sunlight, and Adkins, still in his evil-looking disguise, was hammering on the bedroom door of Elias, and delivering his urgent question in loud and anxious tones : "Is the *Kentish Maid* still at anchor?"

"She was," said Elias, wiping sleep from his eyes, "when I went to bed."

"God grant that she has not taken the night tide."

Elias stretched and yawned. "I do not think so, sir. A dreadful storm has kept me awake most of the night."

"Good." Adkins was positively beaming through his straggly false whiskers. "Quickly, prime your pistols, get that laggard Barker from his bed and have him bring me a jug of ale. No breakfast for you, my friend, or you get Barker to parcel some beef sandwiches."

Elias was dragging on his clothes, infected by the thief-taker's excitement, and Adkins, pausing before going to his own room, was still smiling. There was work to do, and it was to his taste. "While you are preparing," he said, "I shall get off these duds and clean up. This morning, captain, I shall wear my best." Harry Adkins, celebrated and successful, man of fashion, had a sense of occasion.

Now there were three policemen—a thieftaker, a captain and a patrolman, against whole towns and villages in a part of Kent infested with smugglers.

They took both the curricle and the chaise, racing for St. Mary's Bay as the day brightened.

There in the cove lay the *Kentish Maid*, firmly at anchor and no sign of life aboard her.

"Now," said Adkins, "to the skipper's cottage and a long talk with Bartholomew Barley."

* * *

That very morning Susannah Honeycombe had been summoned yet again to the apothecary's shop. At first Quested was all gentlemanliness and gracious bows.

"We shall do another painting, my dear, this time in a different pose," he said.

"I am very tired of it all," murmured Susannah, a hint of desperation in her voice.

"Pity," mocked Quested. "You are such a pretty creature—that is to say, to the eye of an artist."

"I do not think you look on me with a *painter's* eye," said the lady. "I suspect, indeed I know, that you look on me with quite a different eye, and I do not like it."

"Ah, my dear, a little bold today, eh?"

"As I have said, sir, I am getting tired of it. I do not think I will continue these sittings much longer. 'Tis a farce, and you know it. And please not to call me 'dear.' "

"You will go on with it for precisely as long as I wish it," he said, his voice smooth and sarcastic. "Unless, of course, you wish me to tell what I know. You'd be sorry then that you had not done my bidding. Now, miss, enough of this nonsense. Off with your clothes to the waist and sit you on that couch."

Slowly, as though every movement gave her pain, Susannah obeyed.

She sat naked to the waist, her eyes brightening as they filled, and a slow tear trickling down her cheek.

Quested was gazing at her lasciviously. His mouth leered. His eyes lost their sparkle and were glazing over.

The whole expression of his face was changing, as though at this moment he was becoming transformed into a different person. He moved in a shambling gait to the easel and placed a new canvas on it, seeming to cling to it for a moment before turning to her again.

"I think—this time—we will go a stage further—than we have ever gone before," he said, breathing heavily. "This time you will take *all* your clothes off. I wish to paint you—quite naked——"

"I will do no such thing. You go beyond my endurance, sir."

"Quite naked—and in pose exactly of my own choosing." As though he were unconscious that she had spoken he went on talking. "Indeed, I shall place you in the pose I desire of you—with my own hands."

"Go to the devil, Mr. Quested!" Her voice rose almost to a shriek.

He halted as though a fist had struck him, rushed to his desk, scooped a handful of jewellery from a drawer and tossed them into her lap. "Take these," he said. "Take them. They are yours. But do as I say."

"I repeat, Mr. Quested, go to the devil," she said through her tears. "Indeed, sir, I think you have gone to the devil already, and I want no part of it. I do not understand you. You are most strange. I think you need horse-whipping, or that you are ill."

Her fist, holding the jewels, was upraised, and she flung the sparkling items at his feet. "Keep them. I do not want them." She sobbed out the words in fear and anger—and in an extremity of anguish.

His face became contorted. Half-dressed as she was, she rose and flung herself at the door, only to find that it was locked. Turning, she shrank back in terror towards the couch.

"I will remove the remainder of your clothes—with my own hands," he said, his eyes still glazed, his voice soft and caressing.

Very slowly, as though in some strange trance, he advanced towards her.

*   ·   *   *

The three policemen had arrived at Barley's cottage before Susannah entered Quested's shop door.

The skipper's wife, a thin, care-worn creature, answered their knocking, and they brushed past her into the low-ceilinged room.

"Bartholomew Barley," said Adkins. "He is here?"

"Aye," she said in a voice drained of emotion. "He's abed.

Sleepin' off the drink. Who would you be, sir, and why wantin' 'im? I'll call 'im down."

"Pray do not trouble," said Adkins. "We shall go up to him."

"But why? Who be you?" she asked again. "I ain't seen you afore."

"We're the law," said the thieftaker, his foot on the narrow stairs.

Barley lay blinking as the door of his bedroom was flung open. At the door stood two men, pistols in their belts, cutlasses in their hands.

He had not seen them before, he thought, stumbling from his bed, spilling filthy blankets and sheets on the floor.

But in the middle of the room was an elegant, top-hatted figure twirling an ebony cane in gloved hands. And this man he *had* seen before—aye, and ordered a man to hit him on the head one night at the old windmill. The damned Bow Street Runner. What, in the name of the devil, did he want?

"Bartholomew Barley?" The voice rang and echoed with confidence.

"Aye." To Barley it was like a tormented dream from which he must force himself to waken.

"I am Harry Adkins from Bow Street, and I would have you answer some questions—in the name of the law. I warn you that whatever you say will be remembered by myself and these two witnesses and used against you if it be necessary.

"Wot d'yer want to know?"

"Many things. But we shall begin with your ship, the *Kentish Maid*. You are her master, are you not?"

"Aye."

"Does she belong to you?"

"Aye."

"I do not think you have a care for the truth, Barley. But we will return to that question later. In the meantime, what of your voyages to France?"

"France, sir? I don't sail there."

"You do, sir."

"Wot would I be wantin', sailing ter France—a war on and all."

"Barley, do not, pray, think you are going to get the better of this interview. Your ship has been followed to the French coast by a sloop of His Majesty's Navy, and you were seen to make harbour."

" 'Tis a lie."

Adkins shrugged. "We shall see, Barley. We shall see. Now the letter you brought from France."

"You lie." Barley coughed and spat on the floor.

"The letter, Barley. Are you deaf, sir?"

"I didn't bring no letter."

Adkins raised his cane and placed the tip gently against the smuggler's chest. "But I know you did. Do not lie, Barley. I saw you deliver the letter with my own eyes. It was at the windmill, was it not?"

Barley's eyes bulged wide, his mouth gaped.

"You couldn't 'ave——" The skipper halted himself quickly.

"So you admit being at the windmill with a letter? Not that it matters. I was hiding behind bushes and saw it all. Now about that letter, the one from France."

"I didn't bring no letter."

"But I know you did. Do not lie, Barley. I saw you deliver it with my own eyes. Now who was the man you gave it to— the man who waited at the windmill?"

"That I do *not* know, sir."

"Explain yourself," barked Adkins.

"Well, I don't know who he is."

"Can you put *any* name to him?"

"Adams. That's wot 'e calls 'imself. Adams. But I don't believe it's 'is proper name. Now look 'ere, wot are you goin' to do with me?"

"Patience, Barley. Give me all your help—and who knows, you may yet escape the hangman."

The words catapulted the skipper into action. He gathered up the skirt of his night-shirt and made a bolt for the window.

But Adkins was quicker. On the instant he had his back to the window and the shining ebony in his hand was no longer a cane but a swordstick, unsheathed and pointing its wavering steel tip on a level with Barley's chest.

"Jump through the window by all means, Barley," drawled Adkins. "But if you attempt so silly a trick you will run straight on to this little toy. Now, sir, we will continue. Is the man who calls himself Adams the brains behind your smuggling gang? Is he the master of it?"

"Aye." Barley's face was ashen.

"What is his real name?"

"Honest, sir. I do not know. No one knows. 'E pays the piper and we plays the tune."

"Is it he who really owns your ship?"

Barley's eyes fell. "Aye. Damn the man, he leaves me no self-respect. I've got to do 'is bidding."

"Why?"

"'E 'as summat on me."

"What does he have, as you so quaintly put it, on you?"

Barley slumped on to the bed, sitting there dejectedly. For a time he did not speak, and Adkins allowed him silence. "I was a member of a gang o' free traders," he said at last. "It were a long time ago, and it were broken up by the coastguard men. Nearly everyone was taken, but I escaped."

"Continue."

"I'd done nuthin' wors'n 'elp with the runs, but I remember it gave me the scare o' my life. Lived an honest life ever since. Anyways, the gang were all broken up. Then this Adams gentleman got a 'old on me. I 'ad an old bit uv a ship, not much use for sea-goin', but good enough for fishin', long as yer didn't go out too far.

"Well, this 'ere Adams comes along and tells me I must work a new smuggling gang. 'Naw,' I says. 'Finished wi' that caper', I says.

"Then 'e tells me 'e knows I wus once a smuggler. Didn't believe 'im, for it were a long time ago and all forgotten around these parts. But 'e gave me such details o' the things I'd done as a smuggler I knew 'e remembered more'n I'd forgot about it. One wrong move from me, he says, and 'e'd report me to the authorities. Besides which, there was a splendid ship for me, which he would provide, and I could tell everyone I owned it myself, he said. I'd always wanted a ship like that. . . ."

"So, he had a hold on you?"

"Aye."

Adkins waited for a moment, then rapped out his next question like a pistol shot. "Is that why he made you shoot the midshipman?"

"The swine!" Barley was on his feet, trembling with rage. "Is that wot 'e told you? The bastard liar! It were 'im. It were 'im wot shot the middy. It were 'im, the lyin', pox-faced bastard. For Gawd's sake believe me, sir. Bring a 'Oly Bible and I'll swear on it."

Adkins placed a hand on the man's shoulder. "I believe you," he said.

Barley sat down again on the bed.

"Wot will 'appen to me?" he said at last.

"You may get a prison sentence for smuggling. There is, I am afraid, nothing I can promise you—save that I will give evidence that you helped me with my inquiries. It may help. Put on some clothes, and one of my friends has some iron jewellery to put on your wrists. Then you will come with us.

"Now, one thing more. Has Adams yet given you a letter to take to France?"

"No, sir."

"Then he will have it still in his pocket, and we shall go now to take it from him."

"*You* know who Adams is?" Barley's voice was hushed with awe.

"Yes, Barley, I think I do, and now—to Dymchurch with all speed."

CHAPTER TWENTY-SIX

THE PATROLMAN WHO had just joined the team in Kent was left in his chaise outside the apothecary's shop with Barley while Adkins and Elias brushed past Quested's astonished assistance without a word and strode up the stairs.

They had arrived, though the thieftaker did not yet know it, at the precise moment that Susannah leaned terrified against the couch and Quested moved slowly towards her across the creaking floorboards.

The evil genius of Dymchurch neither saw nor heard the turning of the door handle, which operation was found to be useless at the other side. But he did hear the belabouring that followed, and the roar that accompanied it. "Open up—in the name of the law."

The words brought his mind whirling back from the strange personality that seemed to be taking possession of him, and his voice from its insidious softness to an angry rasping. He dragged open a drawer and grabbed a pistol, while Susannah ran to crouch in a far corner of the room.

"Leave the door alone," shouted the apothecary. "Stay where you are or I shall shoot you dead."

"Put up your pistol, Quested, for we are coming in," shouted Adkins. "There are more than one of us and we are all armed. You may kill one of us, but you would die instantly yourself, for we are all excellent shots. Open up this minute."

"Go to the devil!" roared Quested.

"Break down the door," Adkins ordered Elias.

Once, twice Elias crashed the butt of his carbine at the lock. Then one kick crashed open the door.

Quested fired. But the two policemen had leapt swiftly to each side, and the ball whistled through the empty doorway and embedded itself in the wall of the corridor.

Then the two unwelcome visitors were in the room and Adkins was smiling most confidently. "You have spent your shot, Quested," he said calmly, "and I do not imagine my friend, who as you note is well armed, will allow you to re-prime."

"Adkins's eyes swept the room, and his smile vanished. "Susannah!" he exclaimed. "In the name of God, Susannah!" The line of his mouth was as straight as a gun barrel, his eyes flaming.

He turned with rage upon Quested, for he noted that Susannah's skirt was torn at the waist. "What is the meaning of this?"

Quested was assuming a supercilious attitude. "A sitting for a painting," he said. "Just a sitting."

"Well, 'tis your last," shouted Adkins, controlling himself with an effort and lowering his voice again. "But for the moment we shall talk of other things. Free trading, for instance."

"What about free trading?" Quested had made a remarkable recovery from his recent change of personality and from his shouting. He had drawn himself to his full, great height and his tone was arrogant.

"Your implication in free trading," explained the thieftaker, "and the profits you have made from it."

"I am a riding officer—or perhaps you had forgotten."

"An excellent cover for your damnable activities, Mr. Apothecary."

"Get out of my shop, you insolent fellow. I shall get you for trespass."

"Trespass? By all the saints, sir, you are deuced amusing. Damme, Quested, I am going to get you for a great deal more than trespass."

"What, may I ask, are you going to get me for?"

"In the first place for buying a ship for one Bartholomew Barley and organizing a gang to relieve the customs of its proper due—the exact amount to be calculated in all good time."

"You have taken leave——"

"In the second place, for trafficking with King George's enemies, the French, while we are in a state of war."

"Nonsense."

"You have been the means of letters going to and fro across the Channel for one of Napoleon Bonaparte's spies. You have carried those letters in your own pocket. How much were you paid for that, eh? I think money is your God, *Mr. Riding Officer*. But it has also been your downfall."

"I do not understand this rubbish you speak. I am of the most respected in Dymchurch. Ask the vicar."

"He who you suggested, slyly and more than once, might know a little more about smuggling than he might care to admit? Would you try to hide under *his* cassock now? No, Mr. Quested, think again. Mr. Honeycombe is more than you will ever be—a good man and a loyal Englishman. Now the letters from France——"

"Tut, man, what letters?"

"Well, I shall tell you about one of those letters. I was hiding behind bushes near the windmill when our sea-going friend Barley returned from France. Pray do not interrupt me. He was followed to France by a naval sloop. He handed you a letter at the windmill, and you took that letter on your own person to Maidstone, Mr. Quested—or *Mr. Adams,* whichever name you wish me to use."

The apothecary opened his mouth to speak, thought better of it and showed the first signs of discomfiture.

"Do you remember a somewhat dishevelled fellow with a straggly beard in the yard of the *Royal Star* as you sat waiting on a form?"

There was no reply, but Quested's eyes glinted suddenly.

"I think you do remember," perisisted Adkins. "He was

chatting to an ostler. He was, if you will take your mind back, Mr. Quested—or *Mr. Adams*—not of a very considerable height or physique—in fact, precisely my own size, eh? Well, it was *me* in that yard. Oh, do not look so surprised, Mr. Quested, for I took lessons in make-up from one of London's cleverest theatre artists. You delivered that letter to a gentleman who, it may interest you to know, must now be in our custody. And the name of that gentleman—Manners, is it not?"

Slowly Quested sank into the chair near his desk.

"Now there is a third thing I wish to speak of," continued the thieftaker. "The third—and maybe the worst. You will stand accused of the murder of Mr. Midshipman Harrington."

Quested raised his eyes, and the light had drained from them. But he leaned forward and raised a finger. "Is it likely, Mr. Adkins," he asked, and his manner was now infinitely more polite, "that I shot the midshipman? Perhaps you forget that it was I who suggested that you should be sent from London to investigate the murder? If you do not believe me, I think you should pay a call on Fordingham, for he has made a written record of my request."

"A good try, Mr. Quested, but not good enough. I am afraid your luck has drained right out, and the top portion of your hour-glass contains not one grain of sand. You thought your suggestion to send for a Bow Street Runner was a trump card, that it would divert any suspicion that may fall upon your own miserable shoulders." Adkins paused dramatically before continuing. "Perhaps it may interest you to know that we have your poor lieutenant, Barley, sitting outside your shop with his hands manacled—and that he is prepared to swear that it was your hand that fired the shot."

"God save me!" breathed Quested at last.

"I am afraid it is a little late to ask for God's help," said Adkins. "We have another pair of handcuffs that should fit your wrists admirably, and you will be very soon on your long journey to a traitor's death."

In the silence which followed, Susannah Honeycombe, who had silently put on all her clothes again, walked forward to face Quested, looked at him with unutterable and silent contempt—and lashed one of her riding gloves across his face.

"Thank you, Susannah," said Adkins, "for doing what my office does not permit me to do. I shall take you home to your father, for I fear you are in need of some comfort. But before we leave this room, Mr. Quested, there is one thing I would have in my possession, and that is the letter for France."

The apothecary sat as though hewn from stone.

"The letter, sir—or do I have to search you?"

Quested put a hand into his pocket, drew out the letter and allowed it to fall from his limp hand on to the desk. Adkins swept it up and placed it carefully in his own pocket.

As the thieftaker took Susannah home, he tried unsuccessfully to engage her in conversation. But it was as though she had lost the power of speech, and the fixity of her expression was like a grief beyond all consolation.

At the little, roofed gateway to the vicarage he tried to take her hand, but she would not allow it.

"I have to go at once to London, as you will no doubt appreciate," he said, gently. "But I shall return. Remember, Susannah, that I shall return."

Slowly, with still no word, without a turn of her head, like a pathetic queen of history going silently to the block, she went up the winding path to her father's home, to cry in his arms with relief—and to weep on her bed for love lost and tarnished because dear, dear Harry Adkins had seen her as he had in that hellish room above the apothecary's shop.

CHAPTER TWENTY-SEVEN

IN LONDON THERE was much business to be done. With a resignation that did him credit as a soldier of France, Manners admitted several things that helped to clear up certain outstanding matters, but sealed his lips on the subject of whatever information he had sent across the Channel.

"I will tell you only," he said, "that I am Capitaine Jaques Beaupuy, and that I have killed for France—three times."

"Whom did you kill?" asked John Clark. "M'sieur Guy de Rohan?"

"Oui."

"M'sieur Paul Rohan-Marichal?"

"Vraiment—yes."

"M'sieur le Comte de St. Brieuc?"

"Yes. They were traitors to France."

"That is perhaps a matter of opinion," said Clark. "They were Bretons who never agreed to your Republic, and they were bringing intelligence out of France."

"They were working for you," said Capitaine Beaupuy with a shrug. "They had to die."

Confronted with Quested, the French captain said: "That is he. So far as I know his name is Adams. It was he who brought letters to me and delivered others. I will tell you that much, for I never liked the fellow."

The letter Adkins had retrieved from Quested read:

Q01 to A01.   Message A39.
List of points on coast where your fishing fleet will find

*it easiest to succeed almost completed. Hope to send it to
you within the week.*

*Most necessary I receive from you urgently good supply
of money that can be used here, as the man arranging the
postal service is making undue demands for even greater
payments for his services. However, if the great event for
which we pray is not long delayed we may be able to make
him continue to work for us under threats instead of money,
of which I feel we have paid him overmuch already.*

For the time being, however, we cannot do without him.

Your obedient servant, sir,

signed Q01.

The letter was reassuring, for it meant that the French spy
had been captured before he had sent his most vital information.

In addition, Admiral Lord Nelson, that sickly sea-dog who
kept Napoleon from sleeping easily in his bed, and the French
sea commanders from resting in their cabins, was at sea.

The two facts brought to the minds of the authorities the
hope that now the French flotillas would never sail for England.

But one thing was certain. On a cold dawn in London a
squad of soldiers would line up their muskets in a cobbled
yard and quench the life of Capitaine Jaques Beaupuy. And
never again would Colonel Jean-Paul Boussant, waiting
impatiently at the port of Roscoff, receive another letter from
him.

As for Ransome Quested, the traitor, for whom the hangman would have nothing but loathing, his end was assured
even before his trial.

*   *   *

On the coast of Kent, in the coves and caverns beyond the
mist-shrouded Romney marsh, Mr. Customer Fordingham
was to enjoy himself immensely raiding the secret places for
smugglers' treasure.

Poor Mrs. Quested was to find kindness first at the hands of the vicar and Susannah Honeycombe (about whom the tales set about by the apothecary's assistants were much exaggerated), and then from those of the villagers of Dymchurch. She inherited money, not from her dead husband's villainy but from the sale of his apothecary's business. Ceasing to live like a hermit, she learned to smile again and invite folk to tea, in the secluded garden in midsummer and in the cosy morning room if it were cold.

Hackett, the landlord of *The Ship*, was to be let off with a severe caution and a severer fright and become a peaceful tavern keeper with a past.

Barley was to be transported to the colonies.

The Adams Gang was to melt away overnight like snow when winter passed.

And it was to be many a day before another member of the coast blockade was to face a pistol in the hand of a smuggler.

*   *   *

The day came at last when Adkins had time to complete some unfinished business of an altogether different nature.

It was being conducted not in a dark-panelled courtroom, nor yet in a secret cove within sound of the waves' tumble. Instead it took place in what was not yet Darkness Dell but Lovers' Wood, for there was yet no sign of autumn and winter was still far off.

It took a long time for Susannah to bring herself to speak of what still clouded her mind.

"It has been a torment to me," she said, "what you would think of the—of the situation in which you found me when you burst into that fiend's room."

"I am not today," he said, "in the role of thieftaker. I am not asking questions."

"You are not, but there are things I have to tell, Harry."

"If you wish, Susannah."

"You will perchance be pleased to know," she said after a

pause, "that you arrived at that devil's room just in time to save me from something—from what I do not quite know."

"I am glad of it."

"But you will wonder why I submitted to those strange sittings when he masqueraded as a painter. I can only hope you will believe me when I say he forced me to do so."

Adkins took one of her hands in his and kissed it. "I believe you, Susannah, because I want to believe you always."

For a time a memory silenced her tongue. "It began," she said then, "after my mother died. Quested told me he knew something criminal that my father had done. He said that my father had misappropriated church funds, and that if I did not do his bidding he would report my father to the bishop.

"I knew that in a sense it was true. My father was a poor country parson. He did not have enough money to give a fine funeral to my mother, whom he dearly loved. I knew that he had borrowed from church funds to do so, but that soon afterwards he was the principal beneficiary in the will of a dead relative, and he paid every penny back into the funds. No one, it seemed, knew except that devil Quested."

"I understand," said Adkins. "But why should this worry you now when Quested lies rotting in a traitor's grave?"

"I wanted you to know, Harry." Her words were tumbling, her face blushing. "I wanted you to know that Quested did not ever have his way of me—not in the true sense. He got some queer satisfaction out of gazing closely at me and pretending to paint me. He derived some perverted pleasure out of it. Is there such a perversion of sex?"

"There are many perversions of sex."

"Well, thank God you arrived when you did. For I fear he was about to begin a further and a worse type of perversion."

"Well, I did arrive in time, and now I should like to spend the rest of my life helping you to forget that hell-hole above the shop."

She was smiling, and it was a miracle of summer, for every day she had worn her clothes like widow's weeds. "In your care," she said, "I shall forget. But tell me, my dear Harry, does what I have told you solve the last question you might have asked in the case of Ransome Quested?"

"It does," he said, answering her smile, "but in all my days as a thieftaker it was the one I was never going to ask."

THE END